"Care to dance?"

Coming from Michael, the question was a seductive invitation. His eyes never left Callie's as he reached over to turn on a tape.

Mesmerized, she moved toward him, and then they were swaying in rhythm to the soft music. Her arms around his neck, Callie toyed with Michael's hair and strung kisses along his neck. She loved the response she aroused in him . . . and the response he aroused in her.

"Tired?" he whispered into her ear, his warm breath sending shivers down her spine.

"A little," she lied, her need for him having long since replaced her fatigue. "I might even fall asleep."

Smiling, Michael pulled her even closer. "Then, by all means, let's turn in. . . ."

Anne Shorr claims she'd be a terrible nine-to-five employee. For most of her adult life she created jobs for herself, freelancing in theater design and retailing—jobs that would allow her time to indulge her passion for writing.

For All Time is Anne's first romance novel, plotted while she and her husband walked the beaches of their favorite vacation spot, Sanibel. Filling in the story was a project that provided warmth during the remainder of a cold Wisconsin winter.

For All Time

ANNE SHORR

Harlequin Books

TORONTO • NEW YORK • LONDON
AMSTERDAM • PARIS • SYDNEY • HAMBURG
STOCKHOLM • ATHENS • TOKYO • MILAN

Published November 1986

ISBN 0-373-25232-3

1

CHICAGO'S O'HARE AIRPORT was a mess. Thousands of travelers weary of months of snow and ice and subzero temperatures were trying to escape. All flights south were booked solid, and Callie knew she didn't stand a chance of getting to Florida unless she was willing to pay for the frills of first class.

Her lightweight but bulky down-filled coat made her feel especially awkward as she wove her way through the masses to the ticket counter. Struggling to balance her huge carryall, a garment bag and her regular purse, she searched frantically for a credit card. The speaker announced her flight was ready for check-in at gate D12, which was at least half a mile away. Callie sighed and shifted her load impatiently while the person ahead of her persisted in asking inane questions about the food, the weather and the seating.

Finally the customer moved away. Callie slapped her charge card against the cold metal counter, saying, "One way, first class, Fort Myers flight 917, please."

"That flight is checking in now," the agent said, looking at her warily.

"I know that. Do you have a seat?"

"Well yes." He began tapping messages into the computer. "Is this all your luggage?"

"I'll carry it on," Callie replied as she signed the charge slip.

"I'll have to get a verification of the charge," the agent announced.

"Terrific." Callie reached across the counter and grabbed her card and ticket. "You call for verification. Meanwhile I'll be making the half-mile dash to D12. If you find out I'm a crook have the security people meet me there." And with that she was off at a run. Her soft-sided luggage slapping at her sides, she made her way toward the scanner.

Another line. "Excuse me," Callie cried, breaking in front of a startled man who was about to place his briefcase on the conveyer. She gave him her most radiant smile. "My flight is boarding...I'm so sorry and you're just the kindest man." Deliberately she allowed her Southern accent to flow.

The man grinned back and with a courtly bow allowed her to pass. On the other side of the detector she collected her things, flashed him a high sign and scampered for pay dirt. Sonny would have been impressed, she thought with a grin. On the other hand he wouldn't be impressed when he saw a first-class ticket charged to his account. He would make speeches about planning ahead and getting herself organized. She had heard a lot about getting organized from Sonny since their divorce.

The waiting area was deserted when Callie arrived breathless at the counter. The last passengers were walking down the ramp to the plane. The agent took her ticket and reached for a seating chart. "Smoking or nonsmoking? Window?"

Callie indicated her choices noting that most of first class was vacant. She would be able to sit alone and collect her thoughts during the flight.

"Thank you, Mrs. Martoni." Then Callie saw a light dawn behind the woman's thick glasses. "Martoni? I've seen you on TV. You're married to Sonny Martoni, aren't you?" Pure awe colored the agent's voice.

"Not any more," Callie replied, grabbing her boarding pass and heading for the ramp.

First class was all but empty, there being only two other passengers. But that wasn't surprising, given the price of the ticket. She accepted the help of the steward in storing her things. He took her coat and hung it with her suitbag in the nearly empty closet. Beyond the curtained partition, Callie could see the other passengers jammed together, shifting with polite firmness to establish territorial rights in the coach section.

"Mrs. Martoni," the steward said, his voice soft and solicitous, "may I bring you anything? As soon as we're airborne I'll be serving our champagne brunch."

"Coffee, thanks, and no brunch." Callie settled herself next to the window noticing that the man across the aisle had looked up from his briefcase when the steward called her Martoni. Sonny Martoni was to football what Kennedy was to politics—a legendary superstar. She hoped her fellow passenger wasn't another fan of Sonny's who would want to get to know all about him through her. She smiled briefly, then turned pointedly toward the window.

It had started to snow again, and she could see the huge de-icing machine at work on the wing. Callie stretched and, smoothing her calf-length corduroy dress, considered changing her suede boots for the sandals she had in her carryall. She was going to look ridiculous in Fort Myers's eighty-degree heat in boots and a high-necked long-sleeved winter dress.

"Callie Martoni! I thought I saw you in the airport." The voice was female, shrill and irritating. It belonged to Bunnie Keaton. Callie turned to face the tall, large-boned wife of Sonny's former roommate.

"Red. Red, look who I found." The woman had alerted the entire plane, and Callie saw with annoyance that the man across the aisle had settled back with a smile to watch this scenario unfold.

"Well, I'll be damned. Callie Martoni." Red, whose face now matched his nickname, struggled to control three carrot-topped boys who were trying to do wind sprints up and down the aisles. "Callie, how are you?" He offered his huge hand in a limp handshake.

"Fine," Callie replied, then gave up a silent but fervent prayer that they weren't traveling first-class. "It's good to see you," she finished with a distinct insincere break in her voice that had the man across the aisle practically laughing out loud. She shot him a look but Bunnie's face loomed close to hers.

"You're traveling first-class, love? Sonny must have made quite a settlement." Bunnie's smile belied the cattiness of her remark.

"It's an emergency trip," Callie explained. "I had to take what was available." Immediately she was angry with herself for making excuses to Bunnie Keaton.

"Well, Sonny can afford it. He signed one hell of a contract this year." There was no malice in Red's comment. "Give him my best, will you, Callie?"

Red started to move away but Bunnie wasn't finished. "I doubt Callie sees much of her famous husband these days. According to the papers, the divorce was anything but friendly."

The woman gave new meaning to the word *brazen*. Callie reached deep and found her sweetest smile. "Well, you know what Will Rogers said about believing what you read, Bunnie." From the corner of her eye Callie saw the man across the aisle chuckle.

"We'll be ready for takeoff momentarily. Would you please take your seats." The steward had taken two of the moppets firmly in hand and was directing them toward the coach section. Callie flashed him a genuine smile.

"You going to Tampa?" Bunnie persisted.

"No, home."

"She said there was an emergency, Bunnie. Drop it," Red muttered, and dragged her through the curtains to the coach section.

Callie settled back and fastened her seat belt. She could feel the man across the aisle watching her, but she wasn't about to feed his curiosity no matter how engaging his smile was. Resolutely she turned toward the window and watched as they taxied.

Certainly no one else would think of this trip as an emergency. The fact that her widowed mother was considering selling the family newspaper was not exactly big news except to Callie. No matter that the paper had been in operation for over fifty years and no matter that their home was one of the last old island places not gobbled up by developers and their condominiums.

Callie had always meant to return to the island, but first there had been college and then marriage to Sonny, which had included life in the fast lanes of Los Angeles and New York and Chicago. Sonny had taken a career in football and mushroomed it into commercials, books, television and now a movie offer. He had been seduced by the bright lights and brass bands, and when Callie had spoken wistfully of home, he told her they would retire there someday. Just one more season, one more show, one more appearance.

Despite Bunnie Keaton's comments, their divorce had been very friendly. Sonny had been more than fair, agreeing to pay her expenses for the first three years and then make a lump settlement. She wasn't wealthy, but she lived well. She just didn't like living off Sonny. At the time of the divorce she had been hostess of a local talk show in Chicago, but once she was no longer Mrs. Sonny Martoni the management had found a replacement and her show was canceled. For the past two months she'd been out of work, living completely off Sonny's money and hating it.

Then came her mother's letter announcing plans to sell out and move to West Palm Beach. Callie was horrified at the thought of bulldozers leveling her beloved cottage and palms. She didn't know how she would do it, but she intended to buy her mother out and run the paper herself. She had discussed the idea with Sonny. To Sonny, who had the Midas touch, there was simply no problem. To Callie, who had always depended on either her parents or Sonny, the problems seemed staggering.

Part of this was Mickey Brookstone's fault. Callie didn't even know the man, but she hated him sight unseen. She especially hated what he and other developers had done to her island. But her mother's letters for the last three years had been full of Mr. Brookstone. How bright he was. How charming.

How much he cared about the island. If Callie didn't know her mother already had a warm relationship with Fred Singer, she would swear Louise Barnes was infatuated with Mickey Brookstone.

She could just picture the man—graying but trim in his pastel trousers and loud sport coats over open-collared shirts. He probably wore a lot of gold jewelry and a pinkie ring with a flashy diamond. Well, he might have charmed her mother, but he would find dealing with the daughter of Henry Barnes another matter altogether.

The man was an interloper, one of many to come onto the island since it was joined to the mainland by the causeway. He walked her beautiful beaches and nature trails and saw only condos and shops and restaurants. Developers like Mickey Brookstone were responsible for the influx of tourists who had taken over the island.

Mickey. What a childish name for a grown man. Probably some postpreppie with a lot of money, who was used to having his own way.

"We are beginning our descent into Tampa. Please fasten your seat belts and be sure all trays and seats are in an upright position. We will only be on the ground for a short time, and we ask that our through passengers remain on board. Have a nice day."

Callie flicked the release and her chair snapped upright. The man across from her closed his briefcase and fastened his seat belt. He pulled a newspaper from the seat-back pocket and scanned the headlines. Callie took the opportunity to study him more closely, out of boredom at first, but gradually with increasing interest. He was tall and tan and... The words from the sixties song flipped through her mind. She smiled, and at that moment he looked up and met her stare.

His eyes were the most incredibly soft rich brown, and they were looking with amusement into her own gray ones. "Did you want something?" His voice was...sexy. There was no other word for it.

As she did in any embarrassing situation Callie chose to cover with a bravado of impatience. "No. Nothing." She reached for her handbag and busied herself searching through its jumbled contents. From the corner of her eye she could see that he had not stopped observing her. To her relief, the plane just then taxied to the gate and the aisles filled with deplaning passengers, including the Keatons.

Fortunately Bunnie and her brood were followed by a long line of people impatient to be out in the Florida sunshine, so there was little time for more than a hurried goodbye. As soon as the aisle had cleared a fresh group boarded. Several were traveling first-class, and while no one sat next to Callie, an older man took the seat next to Mr. Tall and Tan. Callie found herself feeling a bit disappointed.

Half an hour later she looked out to see her beloved Sanibel and its sister island of Captiva floating like two emeralds in the calm Gulf of Mexico. Every time she saw this view peace came over her. She was home.

The beachboy, as Callie had come to think of the man across the aisle, was up and collecting his belongings the minute the plane stopped at the gate. He wasn't that young, Callie decided—maybe thirty-eight or nine. There was a boyish quality about his features from his unruly blond hair to the slight but engaging gap between his teeth when he smiled, as he did now. "See you," he said, tipping his straw fedora, then he was gone.

When Callie reached the terminal she breezed past the crowds waiting to claim luggage. She felt hot and tired and dirty in her Chicago attire. As she had suspected, it was warm in Fort Myers, and when she stepped through the automatic doors she was met by a blast of warm air that lifted her dark curls to get at her neck.

Her mother was nowhere in sight. Late as always. Callie stacked her luggage by the curb and waited. A half block away she saw the man from the plane getting into a burgundy Porsche, a bronzed blonde at the wheel. As they drove past Callie she saw him throw back his head in laughter as the goddess drove and chattered. So much for fantasies, Callie thought.

"Callie. Oh, Callie," her mother called from the station wagon that had pulled even with the curb. "Hurry, dear, I'm in an illegal spot here."

Callie threw her luggage and coat into the back seat and climbed in front. "How are you, Mom?" She leaned over to plant a kiss on her mother's tanned cheek.

"Now, Callie, just take that worried look off your face. I am perfectly fine—never better as a matter of fact. I'm looking forward to having everything settled and getting away from here. I'm tired of trying to make a go of that newspaper everyone thinks I love so. I've worked hard for nearly forty years. I deserve some time to play and I intend to take it, so don't start."

Callie laughed aloud. Her mother's eyes had not left the road, maneuvering the large wagon away from the airport and into the heavy afternoon traffic while giving her speech.

"Well, what's so funny, young lady?" Her mother shot her a glance. "Don't try to tell me you haven't rushed down here in a mad panic because 'Poor old Mom has finally cracked, and I'd better get down there before she does something strange.'"

"Slow down, Mom." Louise Barnes's foot automatically lifted from the accelerator. "Not the car," Callie said with a grin. "You. I'll admit I came here on the run when I got your letter, but I never thought there was anything the matter with your mind. Can't we just talk about this? You're taking a big step."

"Ha! My exact words when you decided—on your own—to marry that football player, and you were barely nineteen." Louise gave her a triumphant glance before turning her attention to the causeway.

"Touché." Callie smiled. There had never been much warmth between Louise and Sonny.

"And how is Mr. Chicago?" Louise asked, relaxing her grip on the steering wheel and leaning back in her seat.

"Sonny is fine. He's in California. He'll be making a movie this spring. How about that?"

"Lovely. Doesn't he give you any money? That dress is a hundred years old."

"I like this dress," Callie replied defensively. "It's comfortable. As for Sonny...we made an agreement. I don't want his money. If I don't want the life, I have no right to the bonuses."

Her mother grunted and drove on.

"Sonny has paid my bills for the past two years. He'll pay through this year, and by that time I intend to be on my own. If I could do without his money tomorrow, I would."

Another grunt.

"Mom, it was a mutual parting," Callie said softly. "We both wanted out. We both wanted different things. We respect each other for the courage it took to admit that."

Her mother reached across and patted her knee. "I know, dear. I just don't like to see you hurting."

They rode in comfortable silence until they reached the causeway toll gate. Louise flashed her pass and they headed for home.

"San-i-bel," Callie sang softly.

Louise smiled at her, remembering the old family song. "Sanibel," she joined in gaily, "the best is yet to be...."

"The days are always perfect on our island...." Their voices were lusty and loud as they sang the song they had made up during Callie's childhood. At the end of the causeway Callie looked left and saw the old lighthouse rising above the evergreens.

"Welcome home, Callie." Her mother smiled at her and they drove onto the island.

Callie leaned out the open window, allowing the breeze to play havoc with her curly hair. It was home, but it was different. It seemed that wherever she looked there was new development—houses, condos, land for sale. Of course, it had been going on for years. But Callie's visits had been limited to long weekends and holidays over the past decade, and while she had noticed the changes, she had pushed them to the back of her mind, having the more pressing problems of her deteriorating marriage to occupy her. Now she saw just how far things had gone. At least the old Chamber of Commerce building was the same.

Every third sign had the name of her mother's friend, Ellie Dunlop, on it. "Ellie must be raking it in," she said, unable to shade the bitterness that a native would sell off bits and pieces of their island.

"Ellie has done all right," her mother replied. "She hasn't sold out, Callie, no matter what you and others may think. She's as concerned about the future of the island as anyone. But she understands that progress will come and you can ignore it and let it take its own course or you can work to control it. Ellie has chosen the latter. She and Mickey Brookstone—"

"Ah, the illustrious Mr. Brookstone. How is God's gift to Sanibel?"

"Callie Barnes." Her mother's tone announced her total exasperation with her only child. "When did you get to be so judgmental? You haven't been on Sanibel for more than a holiday here and a weekend there in ten years. A couple of times I had to come all the way to Chicago to see you. You've no idea what's really been going on."

"I know that Mickey Brookstone and his like are outsiders," Callie replied hotly. "He's a transplanted midwestern businessman who came here for a vacation and stayed to build an empire. Well, he can't have my island for his kingdom."

"You're going to eat those words when you meet him," Louise said. She pulled onto the gravel drive that led to their cottage near the lighthouse.

"I have no intention of meeting him until it's absolutely necessary, Mother. I'm surprised he hasn't talked you out of this place." Callie gathered her luggage and slammed the car door with her foot.

"For being nearly thirty years old, you certainly haven't lost any of your childlike qualities," Louise said sweetly. Leading the way up the stairs to the large deck and screened porch, she called over her shoulder, "Come along. I have things to show you."

Inside the house was the same. Bright yellows and lime greens colored the large open living room and dining area. The galley kitchen was spotless as always. Callie turned down the hall and headed for her room.

"Not so fast, Ms Know-it-all," her mother called. "This is your room." She led the way and opened the door to the master bedroom suite.

Callie gave her a questioning look and stepped into the large bedroom that had always belonged to her parents. The entire suite had been redecorated with white wicker furniture set against pale blue-and-pink wallpaper with patterns of butterflies and flowers trailing up to the ceiling. There were photographs and paintings she had always loved in her own room now very much at home here.

"Do you like it?" Louise stood just inside the doorway wringing her hands.

"Like it? Mother, it's incredible, but . . ."

"No buts. This is your home now. I'm the visitor. Now change out of those winter clothes and meet me in the living room for part two." Her eyes were twinkling when she waved and closed the door softly behind her.

Callie opened her luggage and began to unpack. In every drawer of the dresser there were clothes—her clothes from before she left for college. In the closet several new dresses and sports outfits hung next to her old favorites.

After showering and washing her hair, Callie chose one of the sundresses. It was bright red with white piping and skimmed her body in a comfortable cool way. She slid her feet into her old leather thongs and went to find her mother.

"Now that's more like it. Come, sit here." Louise patted the yellow-and-green print cushion next to her and turned back to the large glass coffee table. She poured them each freshly brewed iced tea and topped Callie's off with a sprig of mint. "Lemon?"

Callie nodded. "Mother? What's going on here?"

Louise Barnes handed her daughter the frosty glass and then took a sip from her own. "Callie, sit back. Relax. I have a number of things to tell you. Some you'll like and some you won't, but decisions have been made and I am adamant. Once you have all the information then you can speak. Agreed?"

"Go on." Callie was on guard.

Louise took a deep breath and plunged in. "Very well. You know that since your father's death I've enjoyed the company of Fred Singer?"

Callie smiled. They'd been seeing each other for over ten years. The relationship was hardly news.

"Anyway Fred and I have decided to be married—"

"How wonderful, Mother!" Callie set her glass on the tray and reached for her mother's small hands. "When? Soon? But you'll be here—"

Her mother blushed and nodded and held up her hand. "Hold on. Let me finish. Fred and I are getting married this coming Sunday. Ellie wants to do the wedding at her place and I've agreed. After the ceremony we'll leave for a honeymoon out West for a month and when we return—" she paused and gave Callie a serious look "—we'll be living in West Palm Beach, not here." She saw Callie's protest coming but stopped her. "Hear me out."

Callie settled back against the multiple cushions. Her arms were folded across her chest in a motion of protest that was the living image of her father.

Louise sighed and went on. "I know how you feel about the island, and you did seem to be languishing up there in Chicago. So I called Sonnny—"

"You what?" Callie was incredulous.

"Well, he was your husband and you keep telling me how mutual this parting was so I felt he would know as well as anyone what was best."

"How about me? Why wouldn't I have an inkling of what's best for me?"

"Because you have so much pride and that stubborn streak of your father's and you would never admit you needed any help. Actually we had a pleasant chat—Sonny and I. He really isn't so bad."

"What did the two of you find to 'chat' about?" Callie inquired.

"Well, I didn't know what the two of you had settled on financially speaking, and I had to find out if there would be any claim from him on the property. But that's getting ahead of the story."

"Property? Mother, what exactly have you done?"

"I simply transferred a bit of property from my estate to yours." Louise reached for a stack of papers on the table next to her. "Callie, these need your signature. Here is the deed to this house, and these are the papers that give you full title to the newspaper and the building where it's housed."

Callie's mouth fell open. She stared at her mother, ignoring the pen Louise offered along with the stack of legal documents. "You have flipped," she said without amusement.

"Not at all," her mother replied. "I am simply taking charge of my life. I have kept that paper going for the ten years since your father died, and I have done it for one reason—you. I have held on to this house for the same reason. Now the time has come for each of us to get on with our lives. I talked to Sonny, and he confirmed my opinion that you'd come rushing down here to save the island. It's really quite simple."

"Simple? This isn't simple. This is a five-thousand-piece jigsaw puzzle. You calling Sonny? The house?

The paper? How could you just take over my life this way?" Callie was up and pacing, waving her arms in dramatic gestures. "I suppose everyone knows about this? Who gave y'all the right?" Callie automatically slipped into her Southern accent when her emotions went unchecked. She paused in front of the piano and picked up the pewter-framed photograph of her father.

She had his gray eyes. They were usually soft and warm, but at times they could harden into steel. Her dark hair also came from the Barnes side of the family, as did the high prominent cheekbones, the slender boyish figure and the full expressive mouth.

"Callie, please come back over here and sit down." Louise had come to stand with her at the piano. "I can see that I've handled this badly. I was just so tickled to plan these surprises for you that I forgot to tell you the real reason I've decided to do all of this. Please?"

Callie stared back at the woman she thought she knew, but her mother had changed. She was stronger, more sure of herself. Callie now had to deal with the fact that this woman, whom she always thought of as a leaner, had taken both their lives and set them on new tracks. She sat down as she had been asked to do.

"That's better," Louise said with a sigh of relief. She took Callie's hands in hers and began again. "Callie, the way I see it this house, the paper, everything will be yours someday. I've no use for any of it now. Life has been wonderful, but now I'm starting a new chapter. Surely after what you and Sonny went through you can understand that?"

Callie nodded, but continued to regard her mother warily.

"One day after Fred and I had decided to marry, I was trying to decide what to do with all this, how to leave it behind and still hold on to it for your inheritance. Then it hit me. How delightful to give you your inheritance while I'm still alive to see you enjoying it. Perfecto."

The suspicion began to fade and Callie regarded her mother with a mixture of respect and surprise.

"On the other hand, having done it I can see that it was perhaps inappropriate. I mean I've changed and so have you. How do I know you feel the same about all this now as you did ten years ago?"

Tears formed and spilled onto Callie's cheeks as her mother rambled on. "Oh, dear." Louise berated herself when the flood started. "I have blown it, haven't I? I'm sorry, dear. I was so wrapped up in my own happiness and the pure pleasure of the planning that I never thought . . . Well, you don't have to keep any of it, you know. Once you sign these papers you can do with it what you want. Sell it, give it away, burn it all to the ground, though I really would rather you didn't."

"Oh, Mother, stop babbling." Callie laughed through her tears and reached to gather the fragile woman in a bone-crushing embrace. "I do love you.

It's a perfect gift, and I love it and I accept. Where do I sign?"

"Here." Louise guided her hand to the pages and smiled happily as her daughter accepted what had always been hers. When Callie had signed all the papers, Louise handed her the tea glass and raised her own in a toast. "To us," she said. "Two independent women."

Callie drank and put her glass down. "I hope poor Fred knows what he's getting into," she teased.

"Oh, there is one other thing, Callie. Would you be my matron of honor?"

"I would be honored," Callie answered softly. She leaned over and kissed her mother's cheek.

"Then we're all set. There are a million details to work out. For one thing, we must find a decent dress for you by Sunday. Something quite smashing, I believe."

"Is this the part I'm not supposed to like?" Callie asked, smiling.

"What?"

"When we began this conversation you said there were some things I wouldn't like."

"Oh, that," Louise replied, averting her eyes and busying herself with the tea tray.

"Mother, are we talking about a dress? There isn't some other bomb you're about to drop?"

"Well, perhaps just the tiniest one, dear," her mother called from the kitchen. "You see, after our talk in the car I was sure you wouldn't be thrilled to know that Fred has asked Mickey Brookstone to be his best man."

2

SUNDAY MORNING Callie woke before dawn. She threw on an old pair of sweatpants and a T-shirt, and slipped out of the house for a run on the beach. She liked racing along in the semidarkness toward the glow of the rising sun. Sunrise today was an especially meaningful one. Not only was this her mother's wedding day, but it was also the beginning of a whole new life for Callie Martoni.

A few shellers searched the water's edge for the new day's treasures, their flashlights twinkling like low-riding stars. Callie jogged by just as a young woman gave a victory shout and triumphantly held a nine-point starfish aloft for the others to see.

Callie frowned and kept moving. The tourists were little better than the pirates who had once pillaged on the high seas, then retreated to these islands to store their wealth. Too many outsiders failed to understand that taking live shells this year meant the crop would be smaller next year, and so on and so on until there would be no shells at all. Already she was noticing how sparse the crop was compared to when she was a child.

It was getting lighter and Callie turned away from the water's edge to run on higher ground, trying to take her mind off the offending tourists. It wouldn't make sense to lecture strangers who might well be leaving the island the next day. She would have to explore other ways to educate the tourists as they arrived on the island, before they had done any damage.

It had been a mistake to move to the higher ground, Callie realized. Now she was confronted with building after building. There were some that even she had to admit were well designed, but others were less than mediocre.

Where were the clusters of charming cottages that had dotted her beachfront? Where were the swing sets and the multicolored canvas beach chairs? Where were the clotheslines holding yesterday's wet suits? And where were the young families and the old couples in their rolled-up pants and paint-spattered shirts? The artists? The locals?

They were gone, and in their place were these neatly arranged blocks of cement with their rows of screened porches facing the Gulf and their swimming pools in the midst of landscaped courtyards. Color-coordinated lounge chairs in precise rows awaited designer-clad occupants. There were cocktail bars decorated to resemble old island huts, and new restaurants that represented the island's history of pirates and seashells through a lot of fishnets and broken swords.

Aesthetics aside, all this new development bothered Callie. What would happen if the island should be hit by a major tropical storm? It was a danger few people considered; it had been decades since any storm damage had disturbed the serenity of the island. But in those decades there had been an enormous increase in population resulting in overbuilding. Islands were meant to shift and rebuild following a storm but when every available foot was taken up by buildings . . .

Callie was disoriented for a moment. She had just passed the Callahan's cottages, which still survived between two monstrous condo complexes. The MacLean place should have been on her left. Surely they hadn't sold out. She turned and continued to run backward scanning where she had been, trying to get her bearings on this island she'd once known so intimately.

Suddenly a male voice was shouting, "What the. . . Lady, look out. Goddamn it!"

Callie went flying and landed seat first in a swirl of sand, shells and camera gear.

"Damned tourist. Why the hell don't you run forward. It's quite fashionable these days." The owner of the voice wasn't looking at her but was raging about the beach collecting his scattered paraphernalia. "If you broke this . . ."

"If I broke your camera, sir, I will happily replace it or have it repaired. And, thank you, other than a couple of minor scratches, I'm sure I'll be fine." Callie's own voice dripped with anger and sarcasm. She got to her feet and brushed the sand from her clothes and hair.

He turned around to look at her then and Callie caught her breath. The man was none other than Mr. Tall and Tan from the plane. She could see that her identity had not registered with him. He stood silently before her in navy trunks and sockless tennis shoes, his hands planted firmly on slim hips.

Callie righted the tripod and began to dust off the mounted camera. "It seems all right," she offered. This was met by a growl and he continued to stare at her. "Look, I'm sorry. It was an accident, all my fault. My name is Callie Martoni. My family... that is, I own the island paper. The *Press*?"

He walked rudely past her without a word and began focusing the lens and adjusting the settings. When she mentioned the paper he gave her a look and went on with his work.

"If there's a problem you can reach me at the office, okay?" Nothing. Callie was already infuriated by what the builders had done to her beachfront. She had no patience to give old stone face here. "Excuse me, sir. I am trying to apologize and make amends. On the other hand, you are being rude and childish. I doubt seriously that your precious equipment is hurt, but I've made my offer and I'll be on my way." She turned back toward her own house and away from the sun.

"Why were you running backward?" He was looking at her now, all traces of anger gone. She could see the engaging gap between his teeth that she'd noticed on the plane. It kept him from being handsome in the way of the quintessential tanned athletic blond man, but it was a feature that made him eminently approachable. His unruly hair even made him seem a bit vulnerable.

Callie shrugged and looked down at the sand. "It's hard to explain. Long story. You'll miss the sunrise." She nodded toward his camera.

"There'll be another sunrise." He was looking her over now, and Callie suddenly wished she'd been more careful in dressing. The torn baggy sweatpants did absolutely nothing for her figure. "Come on," he coaxed, "what was more interesting about where you'd been than where you were going?"

He smiled at her. She really liked that smile.

Callie's features softened perceptibly and she took a step closer. "It has to do with changes. I grew up here, and this morning I realized I've been away too long. I don't like what's happened. All the construction . . . that thing there, for instance—" she threw a look over her shoulder toward the three-story complex behind them "—it belongs in New York or Chicago, not on Sanibel."

"What have you got against New York?" He grinned and plopped down on the sand, patting the spot next to him.

Callie smiled and sat down. She took a handful of soft sand and let it filter through her fingers. "Seriously, I've been away for a while, and it's amazing how much damage has already been done." He merely nodded and so she continued. "Have you lived on the island long?"

"No," he replied with mock seriousness. "Just ten years, which I'm sure qualifies me as a newcomer."

"Then it's hard to explain. Unless you can know what Sanibel once was. I mean all of this has a certain appeal to those whose only interest is in the future, progress, expansion. To someone looking for a new playground it seems quaint and unique.

"They hurry down here from their concrete prisons and walk around enjoying the land and the sea and the idea of being on an island that's so very conveniently close to *civilization*. The next thing you know, Mr. and Mrs. Concrete Jungle are looking around for a piece of the island to call their own. They put up a house, but they can only get away a couple of weeks a year so they rent it out. Pretty soon they begin to realize there are piles of money to be made because everybody dreams of escaping to an island paradise."

He took up her train of thought then. "Let me guess. When they discover their one house is so profitable, they decide to build another and then they put up a whole complex."

"Yes." She looked at him with excitement. "Take that monstrosity there, for example." Again she jerked her head toward the box behind them.

"Al Mackin might not agree," he said, chuckling.

"How do you know Mackin?" Callie was instantly on guard. Al Mackin had been one of the first of the notorious developers to begin cutting up her island.

The man beside her shrugged and started to dig his toes into the sand. "It's a small island. What you say may be valid, but you still can't block progress."

"Progress is one thing," she grumbled. "Defilement is something else." She saw that he was frowning as if he didn't understand her meaning. "Look, it's just hard to explain to someone who . . ." She let the sentence hang there between them.

"Who doesn't belong here?"

She looked at him then and saw that he had the most wonderfully intelligent and gentle brown eyes. But in the same moment she realized the sun was fully up and the morning was racing by. "I'd better get back," she stammered, standing up quickly to cover the rush of feelings that threatened to engulf her when he leaned toward her. But he was on his feet before she was, taking her hand to help her to her feet. His touch was warm and solid and, as with his smile, Callie liked it.

She started walking backward away from him. "Newspaper office. Monday. Okay? I mean if your camera . . ."

"Callie?" He looked very serious. "Maybe you should try looking where you're going?" At his grin Callie spun around and took off.

A few steps down the beach she turned again. He was standing where she'd left him and he was watching her. "I didn't get your name," she called against the strong Gulf wind.

"Michael," he answered, then smiled and went back to his camera.

"Michael," Callie repeated softly. Another thing to like.

When she got back to the beach house, Louise was waiting for her on the deck. "Where've you been?" she fussed uncharacteristically. "It's only a few hours to the wedding."

"Mother, everything is under control. Relax and enjoy your day." Callie kissed her mother lightly on the cheek and went in to take a shower.

"You're certainly in a good mood," Louise probed as they sat together later that morning. "What gives?"

"It's your wedding day," Callie answered evasively.

"And?"

"And isn't that enough reason to be happy?"

"Callie Barnes, I know you better than that. Did you meet somebody on the beach this morning? Is that what kept you for so long?"

"Maybe." Callie grinned, enjoying her mother's curiosity.

"I knew it. Well, tell me everything."

Callie and Louise settled on two lounges and shared all the details of her meeting with Michael. It was a time Callie knew the memory of which she would treasure forever, this shared lazy morning with her mother.

"CALLIE, ARE YOU READY?" Louise Barnes stood in the living room of what had been her home for over thirty years. "Fred will be here any minute."

"Mother, the groom is not even supposed to see the bride on their wedding day, much less drive her to the ceremony." Callie walked in hooking the satin buttons on the sleeves of her beige lace dress. She pirouetted in front of her mother. "Well, what do you think?"

"Perfect. Absolutely stunning. In fact I think you'll outshine the bride."

"Hardly." Callie smiled as she took both her mother's hands and stood back to look at her. "You're just radiant, Mom. Love definitely agrees with you." The blush that colored her mother's face only heightened the effect of the lavender chiffon gown.

"Now, Callie." Louise's eyes turned stern as she fussed with the high neck of Callie's dress and pressed imaginary wrinkles from the full circular skirt. "You will behave, won't you? I mean there's plenty of time for wars with Mickey Brookstone. Do an old lady a favor and be nice."

"Mother, for you and Fred I'll be the soul of decorum. I won't even pour champagne over his head until after you've left, okay?"

"Callie." Her mother looked worried but just then a car horn tooted. "It's Fred." Louise was flustered. "Now let's see. Suitcase, keys, purse."

"Mom, calm down. I've got your suitcase. Your traveling clothes are at Ellie's. Here's your purse. Ready?"

Louise gave the room one last fond look.

"You'll be back, you know," Callie said softly.

"I know. But it'll be different. I'll be different." She paused for just a second and then turned to Callie and laughed. "Isn't that exciting?" Together they walked down the stairs to the waiting car.

ELLIE DUNLOP'S CONDOMINIUM was on the top floor of a four-story building secluded from the beach by tall Norfolk pines. It was open and airy and furnished with expensive English antiques. By the time Callie and the bridal couple arrived most of the guests had already assembled.

The room was decorated for the occasion with several large airy floral arrangements; the screened porch overlooking the Gulf would serve as the altar. Callie had to admit the apartment was in exquisite taste.

"Callie, darling, how perfectly marvelous to see you." Ellie Dunlop was anything but understated. She crossed the room and gathered Callie to her ample bust. "You look fantastic." Ellie sounded as if she'd been expecting Callie to be at death's door.

"How nice of you to host this for Mom, Ellie." Callie surveyed the room looking for familiar faces. There were a number of old family friends—natives of the island—and several new faces she didn't recognize. Ellie pressed a glass of champagne into Callie's idle hand.

"Callie, I understand you're back for good. Louise tells me you've bought her out—the house, the paper." Ellie's voice was warm, but her eyes said she was taking Callie's measure. It was then that she saw Michael across the room.

He was leaning against the mantel of the ornately carved fireplace. The dinner jacket outlined his broad shoulders to perfection, and he looked as comfortable in this formal attire as he had in swim trunks earlier. She had been thinking of him on and off throughout the day, wishing she'd met him sooner so she might have invited him to be her guest tonight. Now to Callie's surprise and delight, here he was.

"Excuse me, Ellie." She kissed the older woman on the cheek. "I see someone I know." She put her glass down and started across the room.

At once Louise was at her elbow. "Now, Callie. Remember. You promised." Her mother was matching her step for step as they worked their way through the clusters of friends and strangers.

Michael saw the two Barnes women coming across the room. Callie was looking directly into his dark brown eyes. She was a knockout in a pale almond dress that hugged the curves of her body and then fell in graceful folds to the middle of her tanned calves. She looked taller than she had on the beach—probably the high heels of her sandals. Her hair was dark and curly and very inviting. He liked the way her eyes could go from docile to flashing in an instant—as they were doing now.

"Mother, what are you talking about?" Callie could no longer ignore her mother's insistent squeeze on her elbow. She stopped and faced Louise.

"I'm talking about Mickey Brookstone. You promised to behave."

"Mother, I haven't even met Mr. Brookstone. To tell you the truth, I was going to avoid that for as long as possible."

Now it was Louise's turn to look confused. "But you were headed . . . I thought you'd . . . Oh, dear." Louise looked rapidly from Callie to Michael and back. "Is that the man you told me you met on the beach this morning?"

"Yes, Mother, now if you'll excuse me." Callie turned to go.

"Callie." Something in her mother's tone made her stop. "That is Mickey Brookstone. Michael Brookstone."

Michael, unable to hear their conversation, could only translate through their body language, but it didn't take an interpreter to know what had happened when he saw Callie freeze and cast him a horrified look before turning back to her mother. Obviously he had been identified. He decided it was about time to make a move; Callie looked like she was ready to find the nearest exit.

"Louise," he called, making his way toward them. He was calling Louise, but he was watching Callie. Since he'd first seen her on the plane from Chicago he'd been intrigued. He reached the two women and took both Louise's hands in his. "You look lovely. Does Fred know how lucky he is?"

Michael's voice was low and rich and warm. It curved around Callie, caressing her in a way she found all too attractive. She closed her eyes tightly for one second, willed herself to smile, and turned to meet this man who had established himself as king of her island.

"Thank you, Mickey. I understand you've already met my daughter." Louise's voice betrayed her amusement, but she shot Callie one last warning look. "Will you two excuse me? I see Fred beckoning." She gave them each an affectionate smile and moved away.

"Hello again." He was grinning at her as she tried to look anywhere but directly at him.

"You must have had a few chuckles out of all this," Callie said in a sharper tone than she'd intended.

"I beg your pardon?" His puzzled look was genuine.

Callie changed tactics. "So you're the famous Mickey Brookstone?"

Michael grimaced at the use of his nickname. "I really prefer Michael. Mickey is left over from the old days in Chicago. My father is also Michael Brookstone. When we were in business together it was easier to call him Mike and me Mickey. When I came down here and started my own company Michael Brookstone Developers was already being used so I decided to go with Mickey." He shrugged and laughed self-consciously. "And that's probably a lot more than you're interested in knowing, right?"

"On the contrary, Mickey, my mother has told me so much about you, all the things you're doing here on the island. I'd like to know more." With some difficulty, Callie was looking directly into his soft eyes. She had seen the brown centers cloud for a second when she used his nickname.

Now it was his turn to change the subject. "Hell of a party. Your mom is a class lady and Fred . . . Well, Fred's been like a father to me. I'm going to miss both of them. I'm sure you wish they'd live right here on Sanibel." He was studying her again.

Callie was incensed. The man was actually trying to ingratiate himself by complimenting her family. "Of course, I'd like to have them here. For one thing too many of the natives have left the island already.

But then you'd know all about that, Mr. Brookstone."

Before he could answer Callie turned and walked away. She'd seen the bronzed goddess from the airport approaching and knew he wouldn't follow. *Score one for me*, she thought.

"Ladies and gentlemen." Ellie tapped a sterling spoon against a Waterford goblet. "If you'd all gather here near the balcony, we're ready to begin. Callie. Mickey. I need you up here." A tuxedoed man took his place at the grand piano and began to play a medley of Cole Porter tunes.

"Callie, here's your bouquet and the ring for Fred. Mickey, you have Louise's ring?" Ellie, all business, positioned each player. "Wonderful. Shall we have a wedding?" She kissed Fred lightly on the cheek and took her place with the other guests. Louise began to walk slowly toward the minister.

Callie could feel Michael studying her from a few feet away as she watched her mother walk to the altar. Her mother's journey seemed to take forever. Callie chanced one look at the best man but could not handle his intense stare. She made a detailed perusal of her bouquet of pink and peach hibiscus.

"Dearly beloved . . ." The minister repeated the ancient ceremony. Fred and Louise took a moment to state their own vows, and in what seemed like minutes, they were married. "Ladies and gentlemen." The minister grinned broadly. "May I present Mr. and

Mrs. Fred Singer." There was an enthusiastic cheer and everyone pressed forward to offer congratulations.

Callie had tears in her eyes when Louise turned to hug her. "Be happy, Mom. I love you so." She hugged Fred, and then the newlyweds were off to lead the first dance.

"I believe it would be appropriate if we joined them now." Before Callie could protest, Michael had taken a firm hold on her arm and led her to the center of the room. It would have been impossible to refuse without causing a scene and she had promised Louise. She saw the relief in her mother's eyes when Callie allowed herself to be taken into the embrace of Mickey Brookstone.

"Relax, Callie, I promise not to defile a foot of your island as long as you're dancing with me." Michael's lips were close to her ear. Close enough to feel the softness of her hair as it curled against his face. Close enough to become intoxicated by her perfume. She fit perfectly into the curve of his arm.

She pulled herself firmly away from him and met his look. "Consider this dance a wedding present to my parents, Mr. Brookstone, nothing more."

He laughed and pulled her close again. He liked her spirit. This was no demure, Southern belle. The woman he held in his arms was a twentieth-century Scarlett O'Hara, full of energy and confidence. "You are something else, lady. First you run over me and practically destroy a couple of thousand dollars' worth of camera equipment, then—"

"I told you I would pay. . ." Callie's retort was stopped by his lips against her hair.

"*Then,*" he repeated firmly, "you give me your little speech about what used to be and make me feel guilty. Then I find out the lady has a habit of shooting first and asking questions later. I thought Louise and I were friends. What the hell did she tell you about me?"

Just then Fred cut in, and Michael left her to dance with Louise. She made small talk with Fred but her attention was on Michael, who was laughing and charming his way straight into her mother's heart.

After a sumptuous buffet the guests began to gather in small intimate groups. Over coffee and after-dinner drinks they watched the sunset and talked. Callie sat with Fred and Louise and Ellie, listening to the other three discussing their long friendship and the beautiful day.

From time to time Callie caught a glimpse of Michael. He had been moving around the room; now he was talking with several older men. "Investors," Louise whispered.

Occasionally he was seen bent close to the ravishing blonde, his eyes serious and intent. "His assistant, Marlena Davis," Louise provided, and turned back to Fred and Ellie.

"Mother," Callie objected through clenched teeth, "I don't need a play by play on Mickey Brookstone."

"Really, dear?" Louise cocked an eyebrow at her daughter. "You could have fooled me."

Exasperated, Callie got up and moved toward the dessert table. She stopped to visit several old friends, spending a lot of time with the employees from the paper who were anxious to get to know their new boss.

After a while Callie moved out onto the balcony to enjoy the serenity of the moonlit night. She could hear waves prowling the beach and the whisper of the tall pines in the gentle Gulf breeze. She breathed deeply and thrilled to the combined perfume of the salty air and the scent of fresh flowers. She was home, and it was high time.

With an energy she hadn't felt in months, Callie stretched her arms high above her head and clapped her hands softly in delight. She couldn't wait to get down to the office in the morning. There would be changes to make. She would move slowly at first, but soon she intended to make the island news her domain. She'd put her finger on the pulse points of Sanibel and Captiva, and if that meant attending boring council meetings and covering interviews with every mover and shaker on the mainland and in the islands, she would get the job done. "Mickey Brookstone and company, be on your guard 'cause Callie Martoni is home."

"I certainly am glad to hear that.'

Callie whirled around to see that Michael had joined her on the balcony. "Excuse me," she said, and tried to brush past him.

"Not so fast, Callie." He nabbed her easily and escorted her back to the porch. "Ever since you found out who I am you've been spoiling for a fight. Why? Until you ran over me this morning we hadn't even met, although I'll admit I spent the better part of the plane trip trying to think of ways to strike up a conversation without appearing to be a lecher." He grinned at her.

Callie felt a wave of warmth at his admission that he'd noticed her on the plane.

"I was quite impressed to be sharing space with the wife of Sonny Martoni. . . ." The flash in her eyes told him he'd made a tactical error.

"Ex-wife," she corrected him coldly. Another fan of Sonny's. Heaven help her. Someday, she prayed, someone would be glad to meet just Callie.

"Whoops. There's that temper again. Peace. Begin again. From what I gathered this morning and from what Lou had already told me, you aren't fond of either developers or people not native to your beloved Sanibel. And should both enemies come packaged in the same body. . . Well, those poor souls are doomed immediately, no trial, no hearing. Right?"

"Mr. Brookstone, I will be the editor and publisher of the largest paper on the islands. It will be my job to be open and objective and nonpartisan. Believe me, you'll get your day in print." And with that Callie returned to the bright lights of the party. Normally she would not have kept walking away from a debate, but Michael Brookstone made her feel off balance. He was younger and warmer than she'd imagined. It was easy to do battle with someone you could dislike on principle or on sight, but she had to admit that her attraction to this man was leaving her with gaps in her ability to think clearly. She needed time to establish a battle plan, and until then she felt at a distinct disadvantage with Michael.

"Callie," Ellie motioned to her from the doorway of her bedroom.

Louise had changed into her traveling clothes. "West Palm Beach, meet Louise Barnes Singer," she pronounced to her reflection in the full-length mirror. Callie grinned at her and they embraced.

A loud knock at the door interrupted them. "Lu? Let's go," Fred's baritone boomed.

In the living room there was a flurry of activity as Fred and Louise scampered through a shower of rice. Everyone called their best wishes and goodbyes while the piano player struck up a ragtime piece. At the front door Louise turned and tossed her bouquet into the crowd. It flew straight toward Callie. She tried to ignore the missile but a hand plucked it from the air just over her head. When she turned to see who had captured the cluster of orchids and purple violets, Michael Brookstone presented the bouquet to her with a courtly bow and a devilish smile.

The party continued long after the newlyweds had left but Callie was tired and a little melancholy at the thought of the big empty house up the beach. She quickly said her thanks and goodbyes and left, ignoring the pair of eyes that followed her passage through the large room.

Outside the beach was almost deserted. Callie took off her shoes and started for home. Occasionally she passed a couple out for an evening walk or someone walking a dog. She and Sonny had talked about buying a dog, but they'd never been settled long enough to pursue the idea beyond some visits to pet stores in Chicago. Maybe now she would get one.

Callie walked near the surf, jumping back just before the water caught her toes. It was a game she'd played often as a child.

"Hi." Michael fell into step beside her. He'd taken his jacket off and his tie hung loosely over his shoulders. The sleeves of his silk shirt were rolled back to reveal his tan muscular arms and Callie remembered suddenly how those callused hands had felt when she had been dancing with him. His pant legs were rolled, she noted.

"You aren't wearing any shoes," Callie pronounced in surprise.

Michael stopped and looked down. "I know. Neither are you."

"But . . . I mean . . . where are they?"

"I left them back there on the beach near Ellie's place." He started to walk and then stopped and waited for her.

She caught up to him and they continued along the surf's edge, unmindful of the waves that caught them now and then. "Do you live on the beach?" Callie asked.

"Yep, Blind Pass," he answered.

"Blind Pass? You're going to walk all the way to my house and back to Blind Pass in a tuxedo? That's miles."

"What's a tuxedo got to do with it?" That was all he said. They walked in silence then for several minutes. Once he took her arm to steer her around a piece of driftwood she hadn't seen. As soon as they were past it he dropped her arm.

"How long have you been down here?" she asked.

"Is this the interview?" When he saw her eyes flash he held up his hands in mock surrender. "Truce. I came down here for a vacation ten years ago and stayed."

"What about your business in Chicago?"

"My father's business," he corrected, and then simply shrugged. "I needed to get away. There were . . . things I needed to get away from."

"Ah ha. A mystery man." Callie teased a little but Michael did not return her smile. In fact his mood had darkened noticeably. Once again there was nothing to say, and they continued to walk without speaking.

When they were almost in front of Callie's house, he stepped in front of her and took her shoulders, forcing her to stop and look at him.

"I have to be out of town for a couple of weeks. I'd like to see you when I get back, okay?"

Callie gave a little shrug and said nothing.

"Look. I feel like I know you. For years Louise has been talking about you and now you're here, and for reasons I don't completely understand you seem to hate me. I want you to get to know me—and my work—before you hang me out to dry in that newspaper of yours." He was practically shaking her.

So it was business! She was thankful she hadn't let him know how much she liked the idea of his wanting to see her socially. She pulled herself free of his hold. Her voice was tired and flat. "Take your trip, Michael. And don't worry, I'll need at least a couple of weeks to put together my army for this crusade. You should be back in plenty of time to defend your camp." She gestured vaguely toward the large impersonal block of buildings that surrounded her weathered beach house. Without a backward glance she walked across the sand and up the wooden stairs to the deck that surrounded the house. When she looked around after unlocking the door, he was still there.

"I'll call you when I get back," he shouted above the sound of the wind and the tide.

Callie opened the door and went inside without answering. When she looked out from the screened porch a few minutes later, she could see him striding up the beach, his head down, his hands in his pockets.

3

FOR THE NEXT TWO WEEKS Callie was immersed in getting the weekly paper organized and redirected. Her mother had kept it going since her father's death, but that was about it. Editorial policies had gone unchanged for ten years and the reporters were bored. The stories were flat and repetitive.

Callie was especially eager to have a look at recent reports of the council meetings. She discovered that issues she found of major interest and concern were passed over with barely a comment in the newspaper accounts.

"This should have been page one," Callie muttered several times, having come across a crucial vote or hearing.

She tried not to think of Michael Brookstone, but when his name appeared more and more often in her readings she could not fight her memories. His handsome face would flash before her, and she would find her thoughts returning to the last night she had seen him. He had been walking down the beach, his head bent against the wind, his entire posture one of loneliness and vulnerability.

Callie was confused by the sketchy reports she was reading. On the surface it appeared that Michael had on more than one occasion come to the aid of the island's preservationists. Grandstanding, she decided.

She pushed back a dark curl and rubbed her eyes. It was late, and the others had long since left the office. The shops that surrounded the newspaper's headquarters had been closed for hours. Callie got up from her father's old rolltop desk and stretched. She reached for her mug and took a large swallow. Stone cold.

"Time to call it a night," she said softly, gathering some papers to take home, then reaching to turn out the desk light. Only the light from a new moon lit the office as she walked toward the front door.

Suddenly Callie's breath caught. There was a shadowy figure peering in at her through the slats of the old venetian blind.

"Come on, Callie," she said aloud as much to calm herself as anything else. "This is Sanibel, not Chicago." She marched resolutely to the door and pulled it open. "May I help you?"

Michael Brookstone towered over her. All six-two of him was encased in well-worn and tight-fitting jeans and a denim shirt open to reveal his muscular chest. A herringbone jacket was slung casually over one shoulder. "Hi." He grinned down at her. "I'm back."

"Gee, you just missed the deadline," Callie replied sarcastically. "It would have certainly been headline news if only I had known an hour ago." She stood half in and half out of the office. He was blocking her way, leaning casually against the doorjamb, studying her.

"You're keeping pretty late hours," he observed. "Bet you haven't been eating right, either."

The idea that he might really be concerned for her welfare was a little unnerving, and Callie decided to ignore his inquiries for the moment. "Did you want something in particular or were you just hanging around waiting for the early edition?"

"Are you always so flip when you're nervous?" he countered, not moving, knowing she would have to brush against him to get out the door. He wanted that contact no matter how brief. He'd been able to think of little else since leaving her at her house the night of the wedding. He'd wanted to take her in his arms then, but knew the moment was wrong. At this point he'd take anything he could get.

She squeezed past him and pulled the door to the office firmly shut. When she had turned the key in the lock, she started away from him toward the street. "I'll be in the office tomorrow at eight if you'd like to discuss something."

He caught up with her easily and matched her strides. "I like to sleep late. A night person." He shrugged charmingly, maddeningly, and continued to walk with her in silence. "What do you do for fun, Callie?"

"Fun?" She said the word as if it were foreign and needed interpretation.

"Yeah, you know—laughter, let-your-hair-down, good times. Fun."

She continued walking. "At the moment I am trying to save a newspaper—when that's back on its feet I'll consider fun."

"Don't give me that," he hooted. "The *Press* has been an institution on this island for fifty years. You don't have to save your paper."

She flashed him a look filled with anger and something else.

"Ah," he said quietly. "I get it. It's not the paper that needs saving. It's your precious island, isn't it? You have come to do your St. George act against the likes of me, right?"

The night was cool, and Callie hugged her arms tightly across her chest. She continued to walk as rapidly as possible, hoping he would give up and leave her alone. When she felt him place his jacket lightly across her shoulders, she shrugged it away and turned to face him.

"What do you want? Why did you come to the office tonight? And why are you following me?"

"Okay, no nonsense." He put the jacket on himself and Callie regretted its loss. She was cold. "I want you to go out with me for a drink and some music so we can get to know each other a little better. I came to the office tonight because I've called your house since I got home two days ago without an answer until I found out from Ellie that you almost never leave that place. And I intend to follow you until you either agree to let me get my car and drive us up to Captiva for that drink or until you let me see you safely home. Does that about cover it?"

"You actually think I would go with you at this hour to your house and have a drink when I . . ." Callie sputtered.

Michael smiled again. "Actually I was thinking of hitting the Mucky Duck and hearing the band there, but if you prefer my place and a fire and...whatever, that's more than I'd ever hoped for. I'll get my car." He turned and headed back toward the parking lot.

"How dare you?" Callie's voice was low and completely under control, causing Michael to stop and face her again. "You think because I'm a woman you can just waltz into my office and work your way around me until I fall right into your arms and ultimately your bed? Is that it?" She didn't wait for an answer. "I am a businessperson. My business is in knowing what goes on and who makes the decisions that are going to affect my readers. From what I've been able to gather you've been making a lot of those decisions lately. Get your car, Mr. Brookstone. You're right about one thing. It is time we got to know each other better." She folded her arms across her chest and tapped one sandaled toe lightly against the pavement.

Michael turned without another word and walked back to his car. He fired the engine and wheeled in front of her, stretching across the bucket seat to open the door. "Get in," he said tersely, and she climbed into the front seat of his silver Mercedes. She looked around for a split second, and Michael could see she was impressed in spite of herself. But the minute she saw him watching her she pulled a notebook and pen from her shoulder bag.

"You won't mind if I jot a couple of things down while we drive, will you?" Her voice was coldly professional.

His jaw was set, and he looked directly ahead. The powerful car swung onto the road that led to Captiva. For an answer he reached across and flicked on a small reading lamp on her side of the car. He wanted to get to know her better, while all she wanted was a story.

He hadn't imagined her response to him when they'd met on the beach before the wedding. But, of course, that was before she knew who he was. After discovering his identity he knew she'd felt deceived. The truth was, though, he'd been so fascinated by her zealous description of the island he'd completely forgotten to introduce himself. It intrigued him the way she went charging through life at full tilt, her ideals a shining shield.

They drove the few miles to the connecting island without speaking much despite Callie's attempts to conduct an interview. He gave her monosyllabic answers to any question she posed, and if she asked a question requiring more than a simple yes or no, he offered a gruff "No comment."

He slowed the car and found a parking space. The Mucky Duck sat on one of the points of the island of Captiva, and Callie could see as well as hear the pounding surf. She sighed and put away her notebook, then reached for the handle to let herself out of the car.

Michael had started around the front of the car to open the door for her. Seeing her already out, he turned and headed for the music that blared forth from the screened porch of the old weathered building. He always felt slightly uncomfortable with liberated women; he didn't know how exactly he was expected to act.

Hurrying to catch up with him, Callie reached the porch just as the screen swung shut in her face. She opened the door and walked in to see Michael hold up two fingers to the host and head for a table in the corner. The band played on in the next room, and Callie could see they were lucky they were being seated at all. She noticed that many of the locals waved and greeted Michael as he made his way through the room.

"You certainly are well known," Callie observed. She sat in the corner facing the raging Gulf.

Michael sat, also, twisting his chair around until it was very close to hers and allowed him a view of the waves and the starlit horizon. He thought about how like the moods of the Gulf Callie's moods were. She could be quiet and contemplative, and a moment later she might be all spitfire. What was driving him crazy was that he liked both. But he didn't like, nor could he get used to, not knowing which woman was going to show up. He sighed and ran a hand through his unruly hair. "Can we drop this?"

A lot of Callie's irritation had dissipated on the drive up. The truth was she was glad to be with him, to have the chance to know him better for more reasons than just the island and the paper. "Sure," she said softly, and looked at him directly for the first time all evening.

The waitress came and took their orders. He argued that she should eat something but she refused, and he finally settled for two beers. The band was playing a slow rock ballad. "Dance with me?"

Callie took the hand he offered and followed him to the crowded dance floor. She looked up to say something, but he stopped her with one finger covering her lips.

"Callie, stop trying to set ground rules—just dance, okay?" He didn't wait for an answer, but he got it as he pulled her close against his chest and felt her relax and move with him to the seductive beat of the music.

She liked the way they fit, her head just meeting the top of his shoulder. Many men she knew who were her height or shorter made her feel large and clumsy. With Michael she felt almost graceful as he guided her skillfully around the crowded dance floor.

His shirt was soft against her face and smelled of the sea and something deeper, more sensual. She moved her fingers ever so slightly to touch his hair where it met his shirt collar. She was curious and didn't want him to know it, but he turned his face to hers the second she made contact.

"Am I passing inspection?" he teased.

Her eyes flashed, and to stem the tide of her anger, he pulled her very close and whispered in her ear, "Truce, Callie. Put down your boxing gloves."

Callie stiffened, but not at his words. Instead, she was shocked by the thrill that his warm breath, so close to her ear, sent coursing through her limbs. His mouth remained there, and she could feel his breath against her dark curls, caressing them as gently as a sea breeze.

The music ended and the band left to take a break, and Michael led the way back to their table. Callie took the opportunity to make a minute study of his back, the broad muscular shoulders that tapered down to a slim waist and narrow hips. He moved with an easy athletic grace Callie had always admired in men. When they sat down she became aware that he had spoken to her, but she hadn't been paying attention to his words.

"I said, why 'Callie'?" he repeated with the same mocking smile he had given her on the dance floor.

"Calusa really. Named for the Calusa Indians—the original settlers here. They were—"

"I know," he interrupted her gleefully like a schoolboy who finally had a correct answer. "The Calusa Indians, found on the island in the sixteenth century by expeditions of Ponce de León and De Soto. They were great warriors—fierce, brave, cunning. Apparently I have my work cut out for me if you follow your namesake."

"I assure you, Mr. Brookstone, you do." Callie didn't know how to fight the helpless longing she felt when he looked into her eyes with his maddeningly sexy smile. She smiled back, taking some of the edge off her words.

"Mr. Brookstone?" He groaned. "I thought we were getting to know each other. Tell me more about your Indian ancestors. Were they also free spirits? Proud? Perhaps a bit on the emotional side?" With each word he had fallen deeper into the gray depths of her eyes.

"All of that," Callie agreed breathlessly.

"And you, Callie?" His face was very near hers in the candlelight that was flickered by the Gulf wind. "Are you all of that, too?"

She allowed her eyes to meet his. "All of that and more, Michael." She would never have thought herself capable of being so provocative. In a moment he would kiss her. Right here in the restaurant, right in front of many people they both knew. She leaned back abruptly. "Tell me about you."

He continued to look at her without breaking the moment. She knew she was sending mixed signals, and he was confused but she couldn't help that. She was pretty confused herself.

He took a long swallow of his beer and stood up. "I think I'd rather dance. There's plenty of time to tell you my life story later." At the moment he wanted to hold her in his arms, and if dancing would accomplish that he would dance all night.

"I'm not still trying to do the interview, Michael," she said as they moved to the music. "I really would like to know more about you. After all, you have an advantage—you've known my mother for years, not to mention Ellie, and I'm sure they've filled you with all sorts of misinformation about me." She grinned and was rewarded by a definite relaxation in the muscles of his back.

For the next hour they moved together to the rhythm of the small band. Through Michael's eyes Callie saw a very different Chicago—one that had been a boy's hometown, familiar and unthreatening. In return Michael got Callie to tell him about growing up in an island paradise. He laughed at her stories of alligators coming up to the back door following a rainstorm, how she played Huck Finn on the many waterways and canals that crisscrossed the island.

By the end of the band's last set they were alone on the dance floor. Callie could not have put into words what had happened between them. She knew only that she had stopped resisting him and, by the end of the evening, moved as one with him. She put aside her resolution to fight him and instead allowed herself to be captured by him.

Michael paid the bartender and stopped by their table to pick up his jacket. He draped it over Callie's shoulders and smiled when she made no move to refuse the gesture. Indeed she pulled it closer, seeming to want the rough tweed to surround her. He placed an unthreatening hand at her waist and guided her through the room, out into the balmy night.

In the car he turned on the tape deck and soft jazz filled the night air. As they sped along, Callie closed her eyes and relaxed against the deep softness of the gray leather seat. He glanced at her often, though, as he guided the powerful car expertly along the curving road to Sanibel.

She was not beautiful in the classic sense, he decided. Her beauty lay in her zest for life and her hunger for challenge. He had taken little note of her mother's and Ellie Dunlop's ravings about this spirited rebel, chalking their accolades up to prejudice, but since meeting her he was beginning to think they had understated her charms.

She sensed him looking at her, and once his fingers grazed her cheek and trailed down the line of her throat. She felt the car turn onto the gravel drive that led to her house.

Michael turned in his seat and switched off the powerful engine. "Callie? You're home." He was having trouble speaking because she looked so relaxed and peaceful. After all the times she'd turned away from him or shut him out behind a facade of sarcasm and flippancy she finally seemed completely open. He leaned closer.

Callie's eyes blinked open. He was very close. Far too close. She moved toward the door. "Thanks, Michael, I had—"

He caught her face in one large hand, so she had to deal with his nearness. He was going to kiss her and Callie wanted that. Oh, how she wanted that.

"Let's take a short walk down the beach," he said releasing her so suddenly that Callie, still anticipating the touch of his lips, was startled. But Michael had changed his mind. When he kissed Callie for the first time, it wasn't going to be when she was unaware or half-asleep. She was going to see it coming and know that she was being kissed and exactly why she was being kissed.

"It's late," she was saying. "Tomorrow's a workday." She made a great show of taking off his jacket and gathering up her things.

"Ten minutes won't kill you either way. I want you to see something." He got out and strode around the car, opening her door and handing her out before she could protest further. "Put this on." He threw the jacket to her and took off down the beach toward the lighthouse.

Callie followed him, her high-heeled sandals catching in the loose dunes until she reached the tide-packed sand of the beach. For several minutes she practically ran to keep up with him, and her exasperation grew with every ragged breath. Finally he stopped abruptly just at the edge of the wooded path that led to the abandoned lighthouse.

"See this?" he demanded, his arm taking in the entire area.

Callie thrust her hands deep into the pockets of his jacket and nodded defiantly. "What about it?"

"I own it."

Callie was stunned. The lighthouse? They had sold some developer the lighthouse? Tears of disbelief threatened. She was speechless. The lighthouse was the last marker of the island as it had been—as it was meant to be, in Callie's eyes. Without a word she turned and started back toward her house.

"Callie?" She heard him calling her but she kept walking. The tears fell freely now. *What's the use?* she thought. *It's too late. I can't save the island. I should have come back sooner.* She kept walking—a silhou-

ette of anger and defeat against the background of
clear sky and lapping waves.

"Callie?" He had run to catch her, but she kept
moving, brushing away his hand when he reached for
her arm. "Callie," he demanded, stepping in front of
her.

She looked up at him then and saw his surprise at
her tear-stained face. He reached to catch a tear on his
finger. She stepped away from him, shrugging out of
the jacket and tossing it in his direction. "Congratulations, Mr. Brookstone. You have defeated me in one
short evening."

He caught her before she could start walking and
turned her to face him. His hand wrapped itself in her
hair and held her. His other arm caught her close
against him, and he molded his powerful frame to her
slighter one. For one moment she saw the mixture of
confusion and anger in his eyes and then his mouth
found hers.

With both hands flat, Callie pushed against his
chest. She could feel the bare skin at the opening of his
shirt and she had to fight against her instinct to caress
rather than resist. His mouth was hard and powerful
and demanding. He was used to getting what he
wanted, Callie thought with new fury. Well, he
couldn't have her.

Callie gathered her strength and wrenched her
mouth away from his. He loosened his hold on her,

but didn't let go. She challenged him with her dark eyes.

"An hour ago you wanted that kiss as much as I did." His glare dared her to dispute him.

"An hour ago I didn't know you were going to tear down my lighthouse and throw up one of your damned piles of boxes." She met his look.

To her surprise he let her go and started to laugh. He had a wonderful laugh—full and rich and free. "For a newspaper lady you sure do jump to a lot of conclusions. You know, many of us infamous developers love this island, too. Meet me for breakfast in the morning."

"No," Callie answered shortly then started across the sand to the house. "I have to work."

"This is work," he argued. "Breakfast. Nine o'clock. The Café. Bring your notebook." He stood before her, his hands on his hips, his feet planted firmly in the soft sand, waiting.

"Oh, all right. Can I go to bed now?"

"Can I go with you?" The mocking grin was back.

She swung at him, but he caught her arm easily and pulled her to him.

When he kissed her again it was very different. His lips teased and caressed until hers pouted and begged for more. Only then, when he was sure of her acceptance, did he unleash the full tide of his longing. He explored with his tongue the outline of her mouth. He pushed gently against her teeth seeking entry. And she opened to him.

Her arms slid around his shoulders, and her fingers caught and played with his golden hair. He felt her surrender and he pulled her even closer, wanting her to know the passion she was arousing in him.

Her head spun with the embrace, the smell of him and the night. The sounds of the gentle waves against the shore were lost against the pounding of her own emotions.

His hands began to roam over her body exploring the curve of her hips, gliding around to her flat stomach and up until they reached the fullness of her breasts. He found the buttons of her dress and he undid them until he could slip his fingers beneath the edge of her lacy bra and explore the hardness of her aroused nipples.

Callie's entire body was trembling with multiple sensations. Yet even as she arched closer to him her mind screamed for a halt to this, his conquest. Breathless she dragged her mouth away and pushed against him until he drew back and looked at her, his own breath coming in ragged gasps.

"I'll meet you for breakfast—business. Strictly business." And she ran for the steps to the deck of the beach house.

She heard the roar of the car as he sped away and in the dim light of her bedroom she undressed. The imprint of his hands was still on her, and she could close her eyes and recall the full power of his drugging kisses. The problem was, she didn't know if he was attracted to her or if it was all a game to get her on his side. She couldn't be sure until she knew what it was Michael wanted of her.

She knew only one thing. She was dangerously attracted to him, captured by his personal magnetism. And that frightened her a little. She had fallen for charisma and charm once and lived to regret it. On the other hand, Michael Brookstone appeared to enjoy the idea that Callie might be his match professionally, as well as personally.

Sonny had never allowed that. He was the star; she was his shadow. What might it be like to walk next to a man, to share in his decisions and work and ideas? With Michael Brookstone that seemed not only a possibility, it seemed to be what he would expect of a woman. He could become a powerful ally in her fight to preserve the history and ecology of the island.

Who are you kidding? she mused as she brushed her hair and looked out at the Gulf. Remembering the power of Michael's lips on hers, she had to admit that for the moment she was far more interested in what might happen between them as a man and a woman drawn to each other than as business associates.

His smile, his kiss, everything about him told her he was attracted to her, too. "But on what level?" she asked herself aloud as she paced the room. Was it the attraction of a man for a woman, or could his words and kisses be designed to placate her until he could accomplish his goal of bringing Sanibel into the twenty-first century? He had the advantage. He knew a great deal about her while she knew very little about his background.

"Does life always have to be so damned confusing?" she asked her reflection. She would have preferred to have everything in its proper place, including people. If she associated with a person on more than one level, she was always able to separate the relationships, business from pleasure. But so far there were no precise edges to her relationship with Michael. How was she going to maintain and build a personal relationship with him at the same time as she was holding his power to oppose her professionally at bay?

"Watch it, lady," she told herself. "This time you could be caught in a riptide before you know what's hit you."

WHEN CALLIE ARRIVED at the Lighthouse Café the following morning Michael was already there. He was dressed like a construction worker in faded patched jeans and a madras shirt that had seen too many washings. Once again Callie felt her breath quicken as she took in his solid build and tanned face. She walked briskly to the table and stood there willing him to look up from the contracts he'd been studying.

"Have a seat." Michael didn't look up. He was, however, keenly aware of everything about her, from the way she had braided her hair to keep it off her face to the way her T-shirt and jeans fit every curve of her body. He frowned at the contracts before him, but he was remembering their kiss. "Sit down." He still didn't look at her.

Callie sat for several minutes waiting for him to break the silence. Finally she let her exasperation out in a heavy sigh and tried to flag a waitress.

"I've already ordered for both of us. It'll be here in a minute." He started to stack the contracts and reached for a worn leather briefcase.

"You take a lot for granted," Callie said irately.

He finally looked directly at her, and then smiled. "Are we still talking about breakfast?" His eyes traveled boldly over her face and hair and then took a leisurely trip down her neck to her T-shirt.

Callie read his thoughts and felt a blush coming. "I thought this was a business meeting." She reached for her glass of water and sipped it trying to cover the nervousness she felt merely by being near him. When their knees brushed under the small table she practically dropped her water so electrifying was the touch.

He pulled a manila folder from the briefcase. "It most certainly is business." He slid the folder across the table. "I have one hell of a week coming up, and there isn't going to be a lot of time to fill you in. Here's some information on me and my company. After you read that, call my assistant, Marlena Davis. She'll show you around any project you want to see. Then after you've done your homework, maybe we can get this interview over with." His face was serious, and she could picture him in the boardroom making decisions and giving orders. There wasn't a hint of playfulness about him now.

"I see," she said, pretending to flip through the folder. "I really prefer to do my own research."

He shrugged. "Suit yourself. This'll save you some time. Of course, it is biased. I wrote most of it myself. But it's a place to start, right chief?" His mouth remained stern, but there was a flicker of humor in his eyes.

"Actually I have a few ideas of my own," she said, ignoring his teasing. She had planned to take him on a tour of the island, to introduce him to the locals, the landmarks, the environment. She had wanted to make him meet her island as a native, a pioneer, to see it as it had been and should be again. She had planned a bike tour through the bird sanctuary, followed by a picnic at the Tarpon Bay Marina and then long walks on all the beaches from the tip of Captiva down to Bowman and on to the lighthouse.

Suddenly she realized that plan would hardly be conducive to keeping her personal relationship separate from her business relationship with Michael. As a matter of fact, her ideas about explaining the importance of conservation to him faded next to her rather vivid daydreams of the two of them lying on the beach, his hands caressing her body as the sun beat down.

Also, he might misunderstand and think she was coming on to him, rather than offering him an opportunity to gain some insight into her zeal for preserving island history. Just the look he was giving her now said he wasn't ready to take her seriously. She picked up the papers he had handed her and met his gaze levelly. "But my ideas can wait until I've had a chance to study these," she said, and leaned down to stuff the folder into the side pocket of her leather satchel. "Ah, breakfast," she announced as the waitress placed loaded plates in front of them.

The Lighthouse Café had always been her favorite spot to have a big island breakfast. Her plate was piled with whole wheat pancakes, and there was a large glass of fresh orange juice, coffee and sausage patties. She ate with relish and so did Michael.

"Tell me about you and the lighthouse," he said between sips of coffee.

Callie's fork stopped halfway to her mouth and she put it down and studied him for a moment. "I think not," she said, and resumed her eating.

"What?" He was laughing a little, but his expression was one of surprise.

Again she put down her fork and addressed him as she might a none-too-bright student. "I said, I think not."

Now his face registered annoyance, and he also put down his fork and leaned toward her. "I heard what you said, dammit. I want to know what that means."

She started to eat again, looking at him from time to time as she spoke, but seemingly more interested in her food. "It means that last night you caught me off guard for the moment. The lighthouse, as you've surmised, is a vulnerable point for me. I made a slip and I don't intend to worsen it by discussing that with you."

"You're talking like we're some kind of adversaries." He leaned closer now and spoke in a harsh whisper.

She looked directly at him for a second and resumed her meal. "In a way we are," she stated simply and bent to pick up her satchel. Getting up, she said, "Thank you for breakfast and the information, Michael. I'll be in touch." With that she left the crowded room, pausing briefly to speak with people she knew on her way.

Callie spent the rest of the morning touring the village and talking with every shopkeeper and business owner she could find. She needed to get a feeling for what had happened on the island in her absence. It was one thing to go on a crusade, quite another to go on it unarmed.

At two o'clock she took a break and stopped by the office to talk to Jerry, her editor.

"All's quiet," he reported. "I've got the kid working on that story you asked for on the Indians. You really think the tourists are going to want to read a bunch of history and ecology, Callie?"

"I don't care what the tourists read. The *Press* is a local paper, and I care what the locals read."

Jerry scratched his balding head and leaned back in his chair, propping his feet on her desk. "Callie, can a crusty old editor offer his publisher a little free advice?"

Callie looked up from the dummy sheet she'd been proofreading and nodded. "Shoot." She needed the support of this man who had worked for her parents and knew the island almost as well as any native. Not only that, she respected his opinion.

"Sanibel and Captiva have changed a lot, Callie, and not all of it for the worse. I understand you're running a newspaper here and you have a dedication to reporting the news that most affects the island, but you're also running a business...a business that's not supported by subscriptions. That's small potatoes, honey. Your business runs on advertising and if you go off alienating island businesses—most of which, by the way, are run by non-natives—you're gonna bury yourself before you accomplish anything."

"But, Jerry, it's almost too late already. Have you seen that monstrosity they want to build where the Chapman place was? And where are the shells, where are the beach grasses, the sea grapes, the palms? Have you seen this year's red tide? Even the 'gators are having to be hatched under unnatural conditions." She waved a photograph for an article on replenishing the endangered alligator population at him.

"I know. But you've got to ease them into it and that means the natives and the tourists. You've got to find a way to make everybody aware and at the same time let them think it was their idea. The thing to do, Callie, is to somehow get the tourists to thinking about ecology when they first come on the island as if it's somehow their own idea to care for the land. You make them feel a part of the island, not like invaders."

"But dammit, Jerry, they are invaders," she raved, then seeing his look of fatherly concern she settled back in her chair and placed her own feet on the desk and grinned. "Okay, what do we do about it?"

Jerry got up then and grabbed some folders from the file closest to his desk. He spread them before her. "How about starting with a series on the old families of the island—how they got here, who they were, how they lived—the whole bit. Then have the *Press* sponsor some historical days, a festival maybe, get the churches involved and the historical society. For the next several months we run two stories on page one in every issue—one historical feature and one ecology story. Inside we do columns on shelling and preservation and birding. Get Captain Jack over at the marina to do a column, and Ellie Dunlop can give us all sorts of stuff on history."

"It sounds good, Jerry, but what about the builders? I mean the developing will still go on. It's almost too late now."

"Callie." He looked at her, exasperated. "The buildings didn't go up overnight. We're talking about years, not months, and the existing developments won't just go away. Give those of us who stayed and watched a little credit, too, will ya? You aren't starting a new war here, you know, we've been at this for years already. Why do you think there's a limit to the height of the buildings? To the number of units per square acre? Some of us have been here all along. And we happen to think we've done a pretty good job of maintaining the history and flavor of the islands." He turned away then and looked out the window.

"I'm sorry." Callie went and stood next to him. "You're right. I was gone and now I'm here trying to clear up the whole thing in one week. I guess I feel a little guilty for leaving in the first place."

Jerry put his arm around her shoulders. "It's okay, kiddo, we'll get the job done. It's just gonna take some time, okay?"

She nodded. "Okay. Start the historical and ecology stories, page one with the next edition. In three weeks we add a story about the development of the condos and time-share units and begin another series of articles. We'll do interviews with each developer, see what they've contributed, where they live, how their work has held up. If we're gonna educate the tourist, let's go all the way."

Jerry was back at his desk rolling a piece of paper into his ancient typewriter. "By the way, Brookstone's office called a half a dozen times this morning. No message." He looked at her over the tops of his bifocals. "One last piece of advice, Callie. Start small. Hit the smaller developers first until you know the tides. It'll take an expert fisherman to reel in Brookstone."

"I'll handle it," Callie said tersely and turned to get the ringing phone.

"Maybe so," Jerry said. "But I heard you were dancing pretty close at the Duck last night. Seems to me you could be in over your head already."

"*Press,*" Callie announced into the mouthpiece. She reached for her mug to get some coffee.

"Callie? Michael."

Callie froze in midmotion and put down her mug. "Yes." She sat back down; her posture was guarded.

"You haven't called Marlena."

"No."

"Did you look at the stuff yet?" He sounded confused.

"Not yet."

"Look, I thought you wanted to do a story. Do you or not? We're pretty busy here."

Callie's knuckles were white where she was gripping the receiver. "I'm busy myself, but I'm still very interested in doing a story on your company. At the moment we have a number of deadlines to meet, though, and I'll just have to get in touch with Ms Davis when I have the time. Can I help you with anything else today?"

Surprisingly, that made him laugh. The sound was rich and warm. "You, lady, can help me with a lot, though I'm not sure this is the time to discuss it."

Callie noticed Jerry had stopped typing and was studying her over the tops of his glasses. She swiveled her chair so that her back was to him. "Please tell your secretary I'll be in touch."

"Administrative assistant actually." He was still chuckling, and Callie could almost see him, reared back in his executive's chair, booted feet on a huge desk. "How about dinner?"

"No," she answered. For the life of her, she couldn't figure out why she didn't just hang up on him.

"No? Okay. Dancing, followed by breakfast?"

She practically hissed into the phone, which only made him laugh harder. "I'll call you for an interview," she said, and was about to replace the receiver when his gruff, totally serious voice stopped her.

"Callie, I'm not talking about an interview and you know it. I'm talking about exploring this...attraction, for want of a better word, we share. And I'm very sure that you're as interested in that as you are in any interview. When you're ready to deal with that, call me." He hung up.

Callie turned then to see that Jerry was watching her with great curiosity. "I'll be out the rest of the day, Jer. See you tomorrow." Grabbing her bag, she headed for the door, shoving her sunglasses firmly in place.

During the rest of the week Callie finished her interviews with local merchants and got her staff started on the new format for the paper. She set up a meeting with Ellie Dunlop for Friday evening. Although she found herself expecting to run into him, she did not hear from or see Michael.

On Friday afternoon Callie left the office early and decided to take a drive along the Gulf. She'd been

meaning to have a look at the projects Michael had
developed in his ten years on the island and this was
her first opportunity.

She knew from the literature he'd left with her that
his earliest projects were small units nestled in tall pine
forests near where Michael lived. When he had told
her that he lived at Blind Pass, where the two islands
met, she had assumed he occupied one of the weathered two-story buildings she passed there. Each
building was designed to resemble a beachhouse, and
though she knew each held four spacious units, the
architecture made each building appear to be a single
family dwelling.

She headed back down the drive toward Ellie's,
passing Michael's most ambitious project. It was a
sprawling complex of winged and ramped units that
hugged the contours of the land as if they'd grown
there. Grudgingly she had to admire the way the
landscaping had achieved a natural look while paying great attention to detail. Even the sign announcing the entrance was tasteful and unobtrusive. She
couldn't find any fault whatsoever in the place.

Ellie's condominium was also a Brookstone project. Again, each building housed only a few units so
there weren't rows of concrete balconies as there were
elsewhere on the beach. Each unit was set in a stand
of tall pines and surrounded by the lower, rambling
sea grapes. The walks leading to the pool and beach
were wood-planked paths that suited the terrain.

Balconies were screened, but each one was unique, and there was a comfortable homey feeling to the buildings. It looked as if the trees and flowers had grown up around them over the years when Callie knew full well that the buildings had been placed there long after the trees and shrubbery.

"Callie," Ellie called, pulling her into the spacious foyer, and hugged her tight. "You're working too hard. I never see you. Your mother is going to have a fit when she hears how you've been neglecting your old friends."

"I talked to Mom and Fred just last night. They both send love, and they said you promised to get to West Palm Beach this month." Callie kissed the older woman's leathery cheek and hooked an arm around her waist as they moved into the living room.

Ellie had lit a fire in the ornate fireplace. The evenings had cooled off in the last week, but even so a fire was mostly for show. In fact, Callie noted with a smile, the doors to the screened balcony were open and she could feel the gentle Gulf breeze. Ellie saw her take in the paradox and shrugged with a smile.

"All right. Let's have it. What are you up to?" Ellie wrapped her flowing silk caftan around her and plopped down in the midst of several pillows on the huge sofa.

"You already know," Callie said, smiling, and took a glass of white wine from the mahogany coffee table. She sat in a wing chair across from Ellie and took a sip. For the first time in several days she felt herself relax and let go of the tension of her self-imposed battle.

"Word is you're about to go into your St. Joan routine. Honestly, Callie, you haven't changed a bit. I remember in school it was always Callie Barnes at the head of the rebels." She smiled at the memory. "I do hope we old folks have kept things from falling apart completely while you were off in Chicago with your football player."

"You've been talking to Jerry," Callie said with a laugh.

Ellie nodded. "He thinks you might be in over your head, especially—" she stopped and studied Callie for a moment "—especially where Mickey Brookstone is concerned." She noted the flush that rose immediately to Callie's cheeks and heard the change in Callie's voice at once.

"Jerry worries too much." Callie got up and walked around the large open room. "This is really a beautiful place, Ellie."

"Not bad for something a developer has built." Her words dripped sarcasm and she continued to watch Callie. "Let's not beat around the bush. Are you here to do an interview on island history, or are you here to pump me about Brookstone Developers?"

Callie had to smile. Ellie was ever the same—direct. She'd never been able to hide a thing from this woman. "Okay." She flashed Ellie the same smile she'd always used on her parents when they caught her doing something wrong. "No nonsense. Tell me about Brookstone."

"Ah, not so fast, Lady Jane. Brookstone the company or Brookstone the man?"

"You're a real terror, Ellie. No wonder you're such a good businesswoman. Start with the company and we'll see how it goes." Callie resettled herself in the chair and took another sip of wine.

For the next hour Ellie went on like a commercial lauding the charms and talents of the Brookstone company. Callie knew that many of the properties Ellie handled were built by Michael's firm; that was one reason she'd come to talk. She knew Ellie handled nothing but quality. She wouldn't touch junk with a ten-foot pole, and she wouldn't work with anyone but the best. Callie trusted her because she had pored over the island papers from the last ten years. She had finally come to understand that of everyone on the island Ellie Dunlop had successfully bridged the change from the old to the new, and she hadn't sold out to do it.

Ellie had just started to describe the latest Brookstone project to be built at the site of the old lighthouse when the doorbell rang. Callie got up and walked out to the balcony while Ellie went to see who was there. She was surprised to find it completely dark outside. So interested had she been in Ellie's stories of

Michael's rise to prominence on the island, she'd lost track of time.

"I'll just call Henry down at the garage, and he'll be here right away. Make yourself at home. There's wine.... I believe you already know Callie?"

Callie turned to see who the guest was and came face-to-face with Michael Brookstone. Ellie smiled, then disappeared into the kitchen to make the call for Michael.

"Hi." He was once again dressed in work clothes, and this time they showed the efforts of his labor. The shirt was smudged with dirt, and the thighs of his jeans looked as if he'd wiped his hands there repeatedly. His boots were coated with a fine sandy film. "I didn't know you were here, or I'd have had my car break down sooner."

"Henry's on his way, Mickey. Did you get your wine?" Ellie breezed back into the room and slipped easily into her role as hostess. She chose to ignore the fact that Callie's expression was somewhere between surprise and delight at seeing Michael. "Here, Mickey, sit down. You must be exhausted. Lighthouse project?"

Michael nodded and gratefully accepted the fragile wine goblet. There was something so incongruous, and at the same time right, about the way his callused hand caressed the stem, and Callie watched his fingers with fascination. She still hadn't said a word.

"We were surveying all day. It's going to be tough to pull this one off, Ellie." He grinned at the older woman and Callie noted how easy they were with each other.

"More wine, Callie?" Ellie crossed the room and filled Callie's glass. "We were just talking about you, Mickey."

"Oh?" Immediately Michael turned to look at Callie, and his inquiry was directed at her. "Research, Callie?"

"Not exactly." Callie shot Ellie a warning glance that dared her to contradict. "Ellie was telling me you designed this building. It's very. . . nice."

Michael smiled warmly. "Wow, that's high praise." He lifted his glass to her and took a long drink. Just then the doorbell rang, and Ellie again excused herself. Michael continued to watch Callie.

He'd purposely stayed away from her for days, testing himself. He had to admit he had failed miserably, fantasizing about her day and night. His work was suffering, and he hadn't had a decent night's sleep in quite some time. She looked fresh as a daisy, even though he knew she'd been putting in long hours at the paper.

Obviously being without him hadn't disturbed her a bit. "You here for dinner?"

"No. Just a visit," Callie answered, thinking he looked a little out of place, his frame dwarfing the small chair in which he was sitting.

"Good. Let's have dinner." He got up again just as Ellie returned to the room and Callie was about to refuse his invitation. He had seen the rejection coming and turned to Ellie before Callie could have a chance to say no.

Somehow he had to be with her tonight. Somehow he had to get a rein on these feelings of his. He was used to being in charge of his own life, his own emotions. Callie made him feel off balance.

"That was Henry," Ellie said. "I'm afraid your car will have to be towed, Mickey. Something wrong with the transmission, I believe. Henry's down there now with the tow truck. I can call you a cab."

"No problem, Ellie. Callie said she'd take me home, and I'll use the Jeep to get back in the morning. Ready, Callie?"

"What about your Porsche?" Callie couldn't resist the dig. She'd seen him drive away from the airport in the sports car.

"That's Marlena's. Do I get that ride?" He saw her hesitate. "Come on, we could have been there by now."

He had taken her glass and placed it next to his own on the mantel. "Thanks for everything, Ellie. Once again you saved my life."

"Don't mention it. Callie, call me. We'll have lunch next week, all right?"

With the teamwork of Michael and Ellie, Callie was out the door before she knew what was happening.

On the stairs Michael took her elbow and guided her lightly toward the parking lot.

"Wait a minute." She stopped and pulled her arm free of his hold. "I don't have time to go to dinner, nor have I said I would go anywhere with you."

"You'd leave me stranded? Besides, you have to eat." And with that he strode to her car. "Come on," he insisted. "I promise no funny stuff. You're too busy and I'm too tired. Let's go."

Callie stood there, stunned by his brashness, and yet she wanted to go. She wanted to be with him. The truth was he'd been on her mind for days. Not his buildings—him. She couldn't have been more delighted to meet up with him in Ellie Dunlop's living room. Nevertheless, she walked haughtily to the car. "You drive," she said, attempting to sound put out. She tossed him her keys. "You aren't the only one who's tired. It's been a long week."

He drove away from Ellie's, heading toward Captiva, and for several minutes they rode in silence. "I've been waiting for your call," he said finally. "Are you still going to do the story?"

"Maybe." She continued to stare straight ahead, afraid to look at his rugged profile. The only way she knew to protect herself around him was to reveal as little about herself and her plans as possible.

"Being with you I always feel as though I'm waiting for the other shoe to drop. You must have driven Martoni bananas."

Immediately Callie bristled, and before she could respond he reached over and patted her knee. "Easy. No harm meant. He must have done quite a number on you."

His hand remained on her knee for a moment longer and then he reluctantly withdrew it. "Actually," she said softly, "Sonny and I were quite good together until he made it. It was his fans who did the number on us." She was a little surprised to hear herself put that thought into words and downright shocked that she had spoken them to Michael Brookstone. He glanced at her and then returned his attention to the road.

Moments later he pulled into the parking lot of a low rambling building. "How does a seafood omelet sound?" He didn't wait for her answer, but simply reached across and opened her door. "I'd walk around, but it's been a hell of a day and I'm really beat." He smiled and got out.

"Michael, I told you I have a lot of work to do." Callie had to get out of the car to talk to him as he was already walking toward the restaurant.

"Come on. How long can an omelet take? Come on. I need somebody to be with right now." He continued up the walk. Callie slammed the car door and followed.

"Do you always get your way?" she asked with a hint of childlike envy.

"I always try," he said with a grin, and held the restaurant door for her.

It was after nine o'clock, and the place was nearly deserted. Michael seemed to know everyone who worked there, and within minutes they were served two steaming seafood omelets, tossed salads and a carafe of wine. Michael began to devour his meal while Callie picked at hers and watched him.

"You don't like shrimp?" He motioned toward her plate.

"I adore shrimp." She took a bite. "It's my weakness."

"Ah-ha, and is that ecologically proper? Aren't the little shrimpies in trouble these days, preyed on by the dreaded ravenous Chicago shrimp tide?"

Callie laughed. "I made another mistake?"

Michael leaned back in his chair and watched her over his wineglass. "Tell me about your marriage to Sonny."

She hesitated for only a moment and then started to talk. She told him all about their college romance, their plans to spend a few years in the fast lane and then return to the island. She'd never talked so fully about the bright lights and the fame to anyone, not even Louise. He didn't seem to be making any judgments one way or the other. With Michael she was able to talk honestly, without making excuses or laying blame on either herself or Sonny.

Callie noticed they were the only guests left in the dining room. The bartender was stifling a yawn, while the waitress set the tables around them for the breakfast crowd.

"I think we've overstayed our welcome. You shouldn't have let me go on like that," she said, pushing her coffee cup away.

"I liked hearing you talk. I'm glad Sonny didn't treat you badly. He sounds like a nice guy." He stood up and pulled her chair out for her. He handed the waitress a bill, then waved and called good-night to the bartender.

Outside under a full moon they crossed the graveled drive to her car. "Feel like taking a walk?" he asked before she could open the door. Now that he'd gotten her to start talking about her life before her return to Sanibel he was reluctant to lose ground. He'd felt her relaxing and letting down her guard a little, peeking from behind to see if she really could trust him.

"It's really late, and we still have to get both of us home." With that she turned to look at him. He was very near, and backed up against the car as she was, Callie was doubly aware of their closeness.

"We could go to the same house," he teased, but when he saw her panic he immediately backed off. "Another time maybe." He handed her the keys. "Actually I'm already home. I live over there."

Callie looked across the road and saw nothing but trees. "You have a nest?"

He roared with laughter. "Would that help? I mean, surely a man who lives in a tree is safe for your precious island."

Callie had to smile back. "It would certainly make interesting reading in the *Press*," she admitted.

When she looked up again his eyes were soft and serious. He began to trace the outline of her face with his finger. "You know, the other day when you had your hair all pulled back in those short braids you looked about twelve years old, and I had the most fierce desire to protect you. Tonight, though, I think I'm the one who needs protection." He bent then and brushed her lips with his own. When she didn't resist, his hand tightened at her nape and pulled her against his hard chest.

"Callie," he whispered, then kissed her thoroughly, bringing every dream of the past several days and nights alive for both of them. She was grateful for the support of the car; her knees were about to buckle.

There was no sound save the beat of their hearts. No cars traveled the old road behind them. The restaurant was dark, and the waves were calm on the beach beyond. He smelled of hard work and tasted of wine, and she savored the feel of his legs pressed against hers.

"Come home with me," he breathed against her temple.

"No," she said weakly even as her hands wandered over his back and shoulders. He was kissing her ear, and his fingers trailed down her neck and across her shoulders until she was shuddering with pleasure.

He kissed her again then, and this time felt her respond to him passionately.

She pulled his face to hers, her hands kneading his back in an erotic massage. He wanted her. And she wanted him. That was the one thing he'd been certain of in days. But while he would have been happy making love to her in the back seat of her car, he wanted their first time to be very special.

Reluctantly, he took her face in his hands and broke the kiss. "I want you, Callie," he murmured, gazing at her lips, full and pouting from the force of his kiss. Her eyes were heavy with her own desire.

Though she had yearned to hear Michael's words, Callie wasn't sure she was ready. He still seemed such a paradox. The man and his business: the man was soft and gentle; the business dangerous and cutthroat.

Michael's voice broke in on her thoughts. "Are you tied up tomorrow?" Surprisingly he didn't seem to expect her to respond to his statement of desire; his tone was gentle and undemanding.

She couldn't speak, just shook her head, her lips aching for his.

"Show me your island?"

Quickly she nodded and swayed slightly toward him.

Grinning, he kissed her once more—a scorching kiss that held many promises and left her reeling. "I'll be at your house at eight," he whispered, then turned, loped across the road and disappeared into the forest.

Callie stood rooted to the spot. She felt ravaged, and yet he had barely touched her. On the drive home she fought fantasies of what it would be like to make love with Michael Brookstone.

Miles away, Michael jogged the long winding road to his house on the bay. He was enjoying his own version of a similar fantasy—a fantasy he intended to make a reality very soon.

5

SATURDAY DAWNED another perfect day and Callie was downstairs waiting when Michael pulled into her drive. There were two bicycles mounted on the back of his open-topped Jeep.

Michael, looking like a beach bum in his running shorts and T-shirt, called, "Climb in, tour guide. Let's get this show on the road."

She reached across and turned the key; the engine stopped. "The tour starts right here," she announced and, with Michael following, walked out to the beach in front of her house.

Michael looked Callie over from head to toe and liked what he saw. She wore a black romper that looked wonderful against her tan, and she'd wrapped her hair in a multicolored scarf allowing the short dark curls to spill over the top.

Callie stopped in midstride, catching his guilty stare. "This is the Barneses' house, built in 1925 by my great-grandfather for his bride, Anna Shannon, whose uncle was the keeper of the lighthouse. In 1926 the house was partially destroyed by eighteen-foot waves during a hurricane. My grandfather and great-grandfather rebuilt it, and the Barnes family has lived here for over half a century now."

She started to walk farther up the beach to stand in front of one of the earliest condominium projects. Its design was particularly unimaginative and barren; Michael had always hated the condo.

"On this site the Ashmore family built a group of small cottages to house the tourists who were beginning to visit the island. They came mostly to fish and buy the fresh produce, which were of course the two major sources of income for the islanders."

She looked down the beach and watched for a moment while those shellers who had slept late combed the beach for overlooked treasure. Sandpipers scurried among them in search of food. "In those days there were more shells than people by thousands. The ladies wore white cotton dresses and the men rolled up their pastel trouser legs and waded in the surf. Or they played croquet and sipped lemonade in their gardens. Sanibel was an oasis in the midst of a world emerging from its first global war and preparing for the next."

She looked up at him then, squinting against the sun, and he realized that for her the beach had momentarily been transported back in time and she had only just returned to the present. Men and women in Izod shirts, bikinis and madras walking shorts now strolled here.

She turned, heading for the lighthouse. "We won't spend much time down here since I assume you already know this story. The lighthouse was built in 1884, and until the early forties it was lit by kerosene. The Coast Guard took it over and kept a museum of sorts here until a few years ago. Now it's empty. It really is the last true landmark of Sanibel that's left. I'd really hate..." She took off at a jog back toward her own house.

Michael caught up and fell into step with her run. She wasn't crying; he'd expected that, though she'd seemed to get very emotional about the lighthouse. "You'd hate what?"

"Skip it. Last one in the Jeep buys lunch," she called, already racing for the vehicle.

Michael beat her but not by much. The lady was in terrific shape, he thought. She directed him to head for the marina, and as they drove she filled in other bits and pieces of local history, pointing out here and there where a business or home used to be.

By the time they reached the marina, Michael was fascinated with her knowledge of her island and getting more depressed by the minute. She seemed to take particular delight in having him see a tacky, commercial building, then letting him know it had been some wonderfully romantic place or a historically significant site.

At the marina they rented a canoe and started across the bay and into the wildlife refuge canoe trail.

"This isn't the greatest time to be here," she noted as they navigated some choppy waters before reaching the calm of the trail. "It's better at either dawn or dusk. That's when most of the wildlife is around. By this time they've all taken off for the day."

"Is this where they make all those movies where the prisoner tries to escape and gets trapped in the dreaded Everglades?" Michael asked, eyeing the fingers of tangled mangrove forest through which the canoe was gliding.

"The Everglades are farther south. But you're right, it is pretty spooky in there." Callie peered into the shadowy forest of roots and water.

The canoe trip took a couple of hours. Callie pointed out every bird and plant she could, each time making sure he understood their importance to the ecology of the island. Her knowledge and her understanding of the importance of the past to the present impressed him. But he wanted to take her that one next step into the future.

By the time they got back to the dock they were ravenous, and Callie bought them fish sandwiches from the marina shop while Michael got soda from the machine outside. They sat on the edge of the dock and ate in front of a watchful audience of pelicans who waited patiently for any crumb.

Captain Jack came out to visit while they ate, and Callie was surprised that he and Michael seemed to know each other so well. She saw that Jack treated

Michael with a great deal of respect and seemed to listen to everything the younger man had to say with genuine interest. She'd known Jack all her life, having practically grown up at the marina.

"Could I show you a couple of things about your island?" Michael asked when they were back in the Jeep and driving toward Captiva.

"Sure."

Almost at once he pulled into the entrance of the wildlife refuge and parked in a gravel lot near the recently built exposition building. Callie approved of this particular project, believing it could be an effective educational tool for the tourists. The refuge and its scenic drive was one of the few attractions on the island for travelers seeking a diversion. For all the building that had gone on in Sanibel and Captiva, the islands had not yet succumbed to erecting amusement or theme parks to keep bored tourists and their children entertained. Callie helped Michael unload the bikes, and they headed down the road through the waterways that lined both sides of the road. They passed pelicans roosting in the trees and saw several wading birds, though not nearly as many as Callie knew would be there later in the day. She loved the way the pink of the spoonbills mingled with the white of the egrets and the deep green of the mangrove leaves.

They rode slowly over the five-mile trail, stopping often to study the mud flats along the jungle trail or, through binoculars, watch the movements of a particular bird. Once they came upon two small alligators sunning themselves on the bank. They could have walked up and touched the pair, but Callie warned Michael that if the female had a nest nearby she might strike in order to protect her young.

"Women," he said with a chuckle. Then, hoping to impress her with his own knowledge of island ecology, he spent nearly half an hour discussing the refuge's mosquito control project with her. But he made a tactical error when he finished, saying, "And not only is this place good for the environment, it's very good for business on the island." Immediately he felt Callie bristle. "Look, Callie," he reasoned, "you can't go back. What's here is here, and you're not going to change that. Why not make peace with it and move on?"

"Because I don't believe in making the best of a bad situation, especially when we can change the way things are going." She had unconsciously included Michael in her plans to make changes on the island, and he was pleased that he seemed to have been cast in the role of an ally.

"You can't stop progress, Callie."

"You call this progress?" They were back in the Jeep now, headed farther up the island, and she was waving her hand toward a site where bulldozers had upended numerous giant cypress and palms.

"Callie, use your brain. There's no way the island can ever be what it was before the causeway was built. People are going to come here. They have investments here. They have an oasis here. I think the natives have done a damn good job of controlling things."

"Oh, really. Have you seen the traffic on Periwinkle lately? How long will it be before they want to turn that island road into a four-lane highway? And I don't think the natives are in charge anymore. Two-thirds of the council is made up of outsiders."

He whooped at that. "Callie, listen to yourself. Are you calling Sam Malone an outsider? He and his family have been here for thirty years. Even Jessica Warren has lived on the island year-round for the past decade. Every person on that council has been living down here for some time, and believe me they are fiercely protective of this place. I ought to know—I have to go to them fifty times a year, it seems, for another permit."

He turned off onto the road leading to Bowman's Beach. On the way he showed her a beach house that had been upgraded and turned into an old-fashioned candy store. There was a lovely garden around the house and flower boxes everywhere. The shop was a replica of a New England country store. He stopped the Jeep and took her in to buy licorice ropes and jelly beans.

Back on the road to the beach, he couldn't resist pointing out that the place had been falling down when the Masons bought and rebuilt it, making it into their home and business.

"Callie, this is almost the twenty-first century. People have to live—they have to work and eat and be able to feed their children. They even have to take vacations. Things can't be like they were."

"They can be close," Callie said determinedly.

"No. Things change. People change. Are you the same person you were when you left here? No. Well, I'm not the same person I was ten years ago, either. And just like outside things changed *us*—things like Chicago and Sonny Martoni and such—outside things have changed Sanibel. It can't be the way it was ever again."

"What changed you?" she asked, suddenly curious.

"A lot of things. Sanibel, for one. Let's take a walk." He parked the Jeep, and they followed the path across the bridge over a bayou to the beach.

"How did Sanibel change you, Michael?" she prodded as they walked together into the warm wind.

"Many ways. When I came here ten years ago it was for a vacation I didn't want to take. I was angry and frustrated and bitter and drained, both emotionally and mentally."

He plopped down suddenly in the soft sand and offered her the bag of penny candy. Callie took some, sitting down beside him. There were fewer people here, and they sat for some time just watching the waves roll in.

"Callie, I was running away from something when I came to Sanibel. I was looking for a way out. That winter my father had put up another of his high-rise luxury condo complexes in Chicago. As usual he had used only the cheapest materials, cut-rate labor and anything else he could find to save a buck.

"I'd been working for him for the two years since I got my degree in architecture. We'd battled before, but this time I had stood up to him. I refused to have my name associated with that pile of junk. When he put up the construction signs saying 'Brookstone and Son,' I went down there and spray-painted out the 'and Son.' He was livid." Michael took a shell and began to dig in the sand as he spoke.

Callie watched enraptured as gradually the piles of sand began to take shape and form under his skilled hands. "So you left because of a break with your father?" Her eyes never left the castle he was sculpting.

"Not right away. I was married then, Callie." He looked at her for the first time and tried to gauge her reaction, but she was wearing sunglasses and he couldn't see her eyes. "Bette and I got married when we were in college. My father had never approved of the marriage, but all of a sudden he presented us with the keys to the penthouse of this elegant pile of crap.

It was completely furnished right down to the studio for Bette to rehearse in—she was a dancer.

"Bette was enchanted. She'd worked so damned hard to have him accept her, not to mention that a penthouse was like a dream to her. How could I burst her balloon? We took the keys but privately I told my father we would only live there until I could replace it with something else—something I'd built myself."

Michael's sand castle was obviously going to be a contemporary one with flat expansive roofs and wings that gave it grace and the illusion of suspension. He was on his knees working feverishly now, and Callie rolled onto her stomach to watch.

Suddenly he stopped building and sat next to his structure, hugging his knees and looking out toward the horizon. "My father laughed at me. He said that with my fancy ideas about preservation and quality I'd be lucky if I could afford to put Bette up in a cold-water flat. The next day I had my resignation on his desk. I collected what I had coming and started my own firm.

"I worked seven days a week, sixteen hours a day. I hustled for every job I could get. Bette was in a show, and she loved the penthouse, so neither of us was looking for a new place. But I was saving every dime, waiting for the day I could start my own project."

His finger traced the outline of the sand structure, and he continued in a voice so soft Callie had to strain to hear him against the wind and the waves.

"One night I was at the office. Bette had the night off, and we were to go out for a late supper together. The phone rang. It was a friend from my father's office. He told me the high rise was on fire, and that it didn't look good." His hand grabbed huge chunks of the sculpture, and methodically he gouged and pounded at it until it was completely gone, as if it had never been. "The ladders wouldn't reach, the sprinklers didn't work. Bette tried to get to the roof, but there was too much smoke. She never had a prayer."

He ran a hand through his unruly hair and stood up, pulling her with him. They started to walk up the beach. Callie didn't know what to say. She'd had no idea he'd been married or suffered so much pain. To her he had seemed like a god—indestructible, living a charmed life of power and money. All she'd been able to see was that he owned half her island and he was a stranger. She felt shallow and small as she walked next to him.

Michael sighed and looked at her briefly as they walked, but she didn't risk looking back. "They took my father away that night to a rubber room somewhere. He had a total breakdown. I went back to his office after Bette's funeral and cleaned up the mess he'd made there. I paid the debts and fired the bastards who'd been responsible for hiring the labor. I put things in order and personally checked out every project he owned to bring it up to code. Then I left."

"That's when you came here?"

"Yeah. A friend had mentioned it. He had a place up on Captiva that no one was using. So I came. For the first two weeks I lived like a bum, never leaving the house except to walk on the beach. I rarely ate or slept or bathed. I must have been quite a sight. Gradually, though, I started to look around as I walked the beach—all twenty-six miles of it—day after day and I saw what was happening.

"Developers cut from the same mold as my father were invading the place like locusts. The natives had no idea how to deal with the influx. About that time I met Ellie and Jerry and your mother and a couple of others. Among us we were able to set some ground rules and make the council see that control had to be enforced from the start or the whole place would be one large pile of concrete and golden arches."

"How did you start your company here?"

"First I started buying land to keep the others from getting there first. When I had the money I put up the place near Blind Pass. Then the time-share complex and then Ellie's place. Gradually step by step I tried to set the standard for the others. If they couldn't meet my guidelines the council simply refused them permits until they could."

They had come to a pile of driftwood and uprooted trees. Callie sat and Michael sifted through the shells trapped in the tangled wood and sand.

"Do you miss her very much?" She almost whispered it.

He looked at her for a long moment and then answered. "Not so much anymore. The work helped a lot. And then . . . I mean, it's been ten years."

He came and sat next to her then. In his hand was a perfect white sand dollar. Callie hadn't seen one so large in years. She took it from him and turned it over in her hand. "Do you know the legend of the sand dollar, Michael?"

He nodded and took it back. "Yep. Religious stuff. I made up my own. Want to hear it?"

She pushed her sunglasses up on her head to watch him now as the shadows gathered on the beach.

"This is the sand dollar. Money, right? Money is what gives a man his power. But look how fragile the dollar is." With one motion he snapped the fragile shell in half. "Money is only superficial. You have to explore behind the money and see what the man is made of. Inside this dollar—" he indicated the sand dollar in his hand "—are five doves of peace, so the legend goes. You have to break the shell to set them free, otherwise they spend their whole lives inside the shell. A man has to get past his money to be free, Callie. He has to find out how to use the money, not have the money use him. Sanibel did that for me."

"And your father?"

"It was too late for him. By the time his shell got broken, the birds were too old. They'd been imprisoned for so long they no longer knew how to fly. He and Mother spend half the year in Chicago and the other half in California. Dad's gotten very involved in politics since his retirement."

He tossed the remnants of the sand dollar into the air and watched as the small shell birds fluttered into the surf. "Ready to go?" he asked as if he had forgotten for a moment that he wasn't alone on the nearly deserted beach. Together they walked back to the Jeep.

"Will you be going to the historical society fundraiser tonight?" he asked as they neared the turnoff to her cottage.

She smiled. "Jerry and I are covering it for the paper."

For a moment he looked perplexed. "Then it's business," he said almost to himself and frowned. He wanted to ask her to go with him, but knowing her feelings about keeping her personal and professional life separate, he thought better of it. She might feel compromised once they were there, and she realized the part he was to play that evening. He didn't discuss his reasoning, though. "How about tomorrow then?" he asked instead.

Callie was disappointed, but reassured by the fact that he at least wanted to see her again. "Sure. Come for supper."

Looking relieved, he agreed. When he dropped her off he leaned across the front seat and kissed her cheek. "Thanks for listening today, Callie." The innocent friendliness of the kiss sealed the promise of their personal relationship far better than a kiss of passion might have. They had found an easy comfort with each other that day. It was a start.

THE HISTORICAL SOCIETY fund-raiser was the beginning of an effort to save the lighthouse, and Callie was frankly surprised that Michael was planning to attend. On the other hand, he was a shrewd businessman and she knew he would always make a point of knowing what the other side thought and did.

She dressed in a cream silk jump suit and wrapped her slim waist with a wide striped sash. She was very careful with her makeup and hair, telling herself that tonight she needed to make an impression as the new publisher of the island's most important paper. In truth she knew there was only one person she wanted to impress.

Callie called Jerry and asked him to pick her up on his way to the restaurant. In the back of her mind she was hoping that her ride home would be with Michael. He had been all she could focus on since the night before. It wasn't just his searing kisses in the parking lot after dinner. It was the way he had listened and asked questions and been genuinely interested in her ideas today. It was the way he had opened an obviously painful part of his past to her with total trust.

Their first weeks together had been a bit like the sandpipers playing at the surf's edge—the birds skittering away when the other tide got too close. She had been convinced that all developers were the same, that all nonislanders were insensitive . . . and she had wasted a great deal of time. As for Michael, she could only imagine what her mother and Ellie had told him over the years. His ideas about what she would be like must have been as wrong as hers were about him.

But now it was summer and the tourist season was over. It was a quiet time on the island, and she was looking forward to the coming months and getting much closer to Michael.

She heard Jerry's car horn and grabbed her tape recorder on her way out to his car. "What a gorgeous night," she said, indicating the full moon and starry sky as she slid onto the front seat next to her editor.

The benefit was being held at the posh Nutmeg House, a favorite spot of Callie's. Small intimate dining rooms furnished in high-backed wicker chairs and round tables covered in shell-pink cloths welcomed diners with the soft lighting of candles and indirect spotlights. A large buffet had been set up in the center of the largest room and waiters moved among the guests with trays of planter's punch, mimosas and champagne.

The owner's wife welcomed Callie and Jerry and led them to the buffet. Callie was starving after a full day on the beach and helped herself to a plate piled high with shrimps, oysters and fresh fruit.

Seeing Ellie Dunlop waving to her, Callie went to say hello, leaving Jerry to mingle on his own. Ellie introduced her to several members of the society board, as well as some of the other builders and developers, making sure that Callie was aware that these were "new" people who were taking an active interest in the past and future of the island.

Callie visited for several minutes, then excused herself on the pretext of collecting data for her story. In truth she was looking for Michael. She worked her way through the various rooms, stopping now and then to discuss the lighthouse and other matters with various guests. Then she heard his laugh. Turning around, she found Michael deep in conversation with Marlena Davis.

Marlena was holding his arm, her long blond hair brushing his shoulder as she pulled him to her to whisper something that he evidently found amusing. The woman was a knockout in a red strapless cotton gauze dress that swirled around her endless bronzed legs. Michael squeezed Marlena's shoulders and gave her a look of such intimate understanding that Callie felt both a rush of jealousy and embarrassment at having observed it.

"Callie." He looked surprised to see her, though he'd known she would be there. "Callie, have you met Marlena?"

There was no escape, so Callie put on her most professional smile and extended her hand to the other woman. "Ms Davis," she said, and shook hands. Marlena's handshake was firm and she regarded Callie with a warm smile.

"Could we make that Marlena? Mickey said you wanted to do an interview."

"That's right. The *Press* would like to do a major story on each of the island's developers in the coming season."

"Well," Marlena said, "after tonight you're going to have one whale of a story to report." She winked at Michael, but offered no further explanation. "Perhaps you'd like me to take you through our projects in the next week?"

Callie found herself warming to the outgoing woman, and Callie's feelings that she might be a threat were fast disappearing. "I'll call your office," she said, returning Marlena's smile.

"Mickey, do I have to work all night or can we eat? I'm famished. Callie, how about you?"

Callie indicated the nearly full plate of food on the table next to them. "I had a head start," she said with a grin.

"Yes, Marlena, I should warn you that Callie's zeal for conservation stops somewhere short of the shrimp crop. We'll see you later?"

Callie nodded and the couple left in search of food. "Awfully nice to meet you finally, Callie," Marlena called over her shoulder. "Michael's been talking nonstop—"

She was interrupted by a none-too-gentle tug on her arm as Michael led her firmly away.

For the next hour Callie mixed with the other guests, making notes and picking up quotes for her story. She was beginning to envision a series of articles shaping up when Ellie tapped on her glass for attention and invited everyone to gather near the small speaker's platform in the front of the room.

"Ladies and gentlemen, please. This is a night none of us will soon forget, I assure you. I'd like to introduce our board chairperson, Michael Brookstone, for a presentation. Mickey..."

Callie was surprised. She had been unaware of Michael's close involvement with the historical society, and she noted the warm applause that accompanied his walk to the podium.

"Thanks, Ellie. As most of you know, last winter Brookstone Developers purchased the parcel of land that houses the lighthouse and Coast Guard station, as well as the community fishing pier. The importance of that property to the history of the island goes without saying and I think—I hope—you know by now that my company's dedication to this island and its future is sincere." He was looking straight at Callie. "After living here for the past ten years, I've come to think of Sanibel as my home, and along with many of you who have been here all your lives, I've been working hard to see that the very special flavor that is Sanibel and Captiva is maintained and preserved.

For that reason I felt that a historical society meeting was the perfect place to unveil my plans for development of the lighthouse property."

He moved to the table and pulled off the cloth. There was an audible gasp in the room as everyone pressed forward to see the scale model of the project he'd revealed. Callie saw that both the lighthouse and station were intact. The fishing pier was there, too, though made bigger, wider and safer. The lighthouse was the focal point but several other buildings seemed to be an intricate part of the landscape of beaches, dunes and pines. This project was going to cost a fortune, Callie guessed, and wondered what it would cost to purchase two weeks of time-share in one of these units.

"The lighthouse will be upgraded and serve as an observation tower for the public. We'll install an elevator and a deck up here with benches. The light will work, of course. The station here will become a restaurant and shopping complex. The galleries or shops will feature only the work of local artisans and visiting writers, painters, designers, and so on, who will live here, in the colony." He pointed to one of the low buildings on the Gulf side of the complex. "Over here on the bay will be town houses and condos for the faculty and staff and back here are the studios and classrooms and the performing arts center. The board of the historical society has voted to take on the Lighthouse Colony as a major project for fund raising this year. In light of that, it will be my pleasure to donate the project to the island upon completion, with the stipulation that it is to be maintained as a haven for the arts."

There was a moment of silence before the room erupted into thunderous applause and everyone tried to ask Michael questions and express gratitude and support. Callie was stunned, rooted to her spot, unmindful that her tape recorder was still running.

Above the heads of the well-wishers Callie saw Michael's eyes search the room until they locked on hers. He smiled then and excused himself from the throng to make his way across the room to where she stood. "How am I doing, coach?"

"That's quite a gesture, Michael."

"A gesture! You call that a gesture? You're tough to please, lady."

"Don't try to con me, Michael. You didn't come up with this idea because of me."

"No, you're right. I'd planned to make the lighthouse special from the beginning, but you can take credit for some of the inspiration anyway."

Abruptly changing the subject, Callie asked, "Do you really have that kind of money?"

He laughed loud and long. "You're awfully direct. Is that thing running?" He gestured toward the recorder in her hand. When she nodded he leaned close to the microphone. "The source of the money is very suspicious. Some might even say there are mob ties."

"Michael." Callie switched off the recorder. "Be serious. This is a big story."

"Okay, turn it back on." He waited and then his voice changed, the gently teasing tones he'd used turned strictly business. "Funding for the project will come from a number of resources including the estates of Michael Brookstone, Senior, and his wife, the former Mary Scott McCallum."

Callie recognized the name of one of the wealthiest families in the country. "You're related to the McCallums?"

"My mother is a McCallum and my grandfather is *the* Alfred McCallum III. Impressed?" He grinned.

Callie knew that family could support a dozen lighthouse projects and never feel it financially. "So you got the money from your relatives," she pressed.

"Some of it," he corrected. "The rest is coming from my company and other donors, as well as a few private foundations such as—"

Just then Marlena appeared at his side, a worried frown marring her flawless face. With her was a man who seemed vaguely familiar to Callie, although she was sure she'd never met him in person. She tried to recall if she had perhaps seen a news article about him. Marlena cleared up the mystery.

"Mickey, Al Mackin has been trying to get a word with you all evening." Her voice was bright, but she looked distinctly uncomfortable.

Mackin took a cigar from his pocket, bit off the end and looked unblinkingly up at his rival. "Good work, Brookstone. The permit meeting is less than six weeks away. Your dad seems to have taught you a lot about the importance of maintaining high visibility and good PR. I'd like to discuss the Mackin Wing of this lighthouse thing."

"As I explained before, Al, there will be no individual wings or honored areas of the project. The entire complex will be dedicated to the people of Sanibel, and there will be a list of donors prominently displayed in the lobby of the theater."

"Keeping the whole thing for yourself, right? Smart, Brookstone, very cagey." Scowling, the man puffed furiously on his cigar.

Marlena looked tense, and Callie was spellbound by this little drama being played out. It was as if the two men were alone in the room until Al Mackin took note of her for the first time. He glanced at the notebook and tape recorder, then glared at her. "Who are you?" he demanded.

"Al Mackin, allow me to present Ms Calusa Barnes," Michael offered before Callie had the chance to open her mouth. "Ms Barnes is, as you know, a very influential citizen here on the island. She not only owns the *Press*, but her family was among the original settlers here."

"I thought your name was Martoni," Marlena said, grabbing at anything to break the silence that had descended after Michael's introduction.

"Martoni?" Mackin boomed. "The football player?"

"Yes," Callie said, smiling sweetly, and offered her hand. "I'm glad to finally meet you, Mr. Mackin. I've been reading quite a bit about you and I've noticed your, uh, work here on the island." From the corner of her eye she saw Michael stifling a smile.

"Sonny Martoni?" The older man ignored her reference to his building. "The man was the best thing to hit the NFL in decades."

"I'm sure he would agree with you, and I'll tell him he has another fan the next time we speak."

"Isn't he here?" Mackin craned his neck to search the room.

"No, I'm afraid not. Sonny's in L.A. making a movie. We're divorced, Mr. Mackin."

"Oh." Callie saw the familiar shutter of disinterest close over Mackin's eyes once he realized she couldn't provide him access to his hero. He turned his attention to Michael and Marlena. "Well, time to party. Right, Brookstone? Mick, this is your night. I have to hand it to you, you really pulled this one off at the right time. You should be dancing, Mick. Get out there." He pushed Marlena and Michael toward the dance floor and pulled Callie along. "Little lady, how about getting some pictures here—it'll be just the ticket for that newspaper of yours, won't it now?"

Loudly he organized the picture taking, ordering the band to play something soft and sexy as he staged Marlena and Michael in a clinch and grabbed Ellie to be his own partner. "Get a shot of this, honey," he called to Callie, and motioned to where the two couples were dancing cheek to cheek on the crowded floor. "Hell of a handsome couple, aren't they? Put that picture front page, missy. Trust me, I know how to sell anything."

Callie bit her tongue and directed her photographer to get the picture. "Thank you, Mr. Mackin. It'll be a fine shot for the society page. Trust *me*, hard news is what sells newspapers on the front page. I learned that from *my* daddy." As she turned on her heel she saw Ellie raise her eyes to the ceiling while Michael broke out in a delighted grin.

6

"AM I STILL INVITED for dinner?" The sound of Michael's voice on the phone brought Callie totally awake.

"Michael," she said, sleepily groping for the clock. "Michael, it's five a.m.!"

"I know. I couldn't sleep."

"So you figured why should anyone else sleep?"

"Whoa!" he said with a chuckle. "The lady is bitchy when she's wakened. I'll have to remember that. Am I to assume dinner is off?"

"No. We'll still do dinner. We can finally get to that interview." She was wide awake now and sitting cross-legged on the rumpled bed.

"Subtle, aren't you? We'll call it a business dinner then?"

"I thought you preferred those," she teased.

"Okay, business it is. But you'll have to come to my place."

Callie had already shopped for their dinner. "Why?" she asked, a bit dismayed.

"Because surely an ace reporter, editor, publisher like you wants to get the whole story. Brookstone at home, on his own turf. The real Brookstone."

"At home in your tree?"

"Right. So bring your tape recorder and your suit and be here at seven, okay?" His voice had lowered to a seductive tone that left her with goose bumps.

"Why would I need a swimsuit?"

"Because I have the most marvelous pool . . . But of course, an old island native like you probably prefers skinny-dipping. Terrific. . . . Are you blushing yet? I love it when you blush. You are, aren't you?"

She laughed softly and put a hand to her flaming cheek. "Is this the way you conduct all your business? No wonder you're so successful. You just turn on that Brookstone charm and pull the nearest female onto the dance floor."

"You were jealous," he crowed.

"I was not."

"Really? Not even the slightest bit? Damn, and I worked so hard at it." After a pause during which Callie sputtered her indignation, Michael continued in a more serious tone. "If you hadn't left so soon you would have seen that I spent the rest of the evening organizing backers for the Colony Foundation. I thought you were there to get a story, but you left before you had a chance. Did Mackin really get to you?"

"Jerry got the story. I had . . . a call. I had to leave."

"Right. So, are you coming here tonight or not?"

"All right, but we're doing the interview first."

"Sure. Callie?" His voice had gone soft and low again. "You looked fantastic tonight."

She treasured the compliment from him, but she'd never known how to accept such praise. "Last night actually, and I'm going to look like hell tonight if you don't let me get some sleep."

"Don't you know why I couldn't sleep?" His voice did not tease. He was very serious.

"No," she answered, almost afraid to hear his reason.

"I was thinking," he replied. "It occurred to me that it would be easy for me to fall in love with you." He paused, said a soft good-night and hung up.

Callie sat for several seconds with the dead phone buzzing in her ear. She didn't know whether he had been serious or if he was simply flirting. But, she reasoned, Michael would never be casual about using the word *love*. She started to smile, then gave a war whoop and danced on the bed, flinging pillows in the air.

He hadn't said he loved her. He'd said he *could* love her. Well, it was a start and she intended to do her part to help things along. She caught her reflection in the mirror and stopped.

"If you want it to happen, missy, what does that mean? That you love him? You've gone and done it, haven't you?" With a delighted smile she went to her closet and pulled out every swimsuit she owned.

For the next hour she tried to decide what to wear, finally settling on a black maillot with a lace insert at the deep V-neck. She chose a circular black skirt to wear over it, and decided to take along a white gauze blouse to wear with the skirt during dinner.

"A little obvious, Callie," she told her reflection, but she stuck with her choice.

That Sunday was the longest day of Callie's life. She walked the beach, thoroughly exploring the lighthouse property and trying to envision the model she'd seen the night before. In the late afternoon she fell asleep on the screened porch that overlooked the beach, and it was nearly six o'clock when she woke in a panic.

Though she raced to get ready, by the time she'd dressed and driven to Blind Pass, she was late. It was almost seven-thirty when she turned onto the gravel road she assumed led to his house. The drive followed the bayou, then turned off to run beside the rows of pines that swayed in the dusk breezes. At last she caught a glimpse of the house and stopped the car to take it all in.

The house was straight out of a Fitzgerald novel, with white lattice trim against the gray cypress walls. Three stories soared in a complex design of porches and gables. As she drove closer she could see a large yacht docked at the pier and a tennis court.

After parking in the circular drive she walked up the steps. The front porch was huge, wrapping itself around half the house. Completely screened against the mosquitoes, it was furnished with white wicker rockers, swings and chaise lounges. There were at least a dozen large potted palms and countless hanging baskets of ferns and flowering plants. Callie was captivated.

Standing before the large front door, she twisted the knob of the old-fashioned Victorian bell and heard a dingling in the house. The quaint bell was a simple touch, but one that made her smile.

Through the etched glass on either side of the door she saw Michael approach. "You're late," he announced with a smile and pulled her into the hallway. He was wearing only a pair of tan swim trunks, and the nearness of his unclothed body was playing havoc with Callie's ability to act the part of a simple dinner guest. Her arm brushed against his bare chest as he led her into the massive foyer.

"I'm sorry. I . . ." She started to apologize but she wasn't sure whether she was apologizing for being late or for touching him. She tried to look anywhere but at his tanned body. The magnificence of his house began to register. "Michael, for heaven's sake, how many people do you have living here?"

He grinned. "Just me. A housekeeper comes in during the week. A little much, huh?" He trailed after her, taking pleasure in her delight as she explored.

"Do you ever use all of this?" She was peeking into the dining room, which was surprisingly contemporary in feel given that all the furnishings were antique.

"Not really. But I'm an architect, and I figured if I didn't build my dream house for me who would I build it for? A couple of times I've thrown parties for investors or potential clients. It does seem like a waste, I guess, but I love it."

"I can see why." She crossed the hall and pushed open a sliding door to the living room. "Oh," she gasped, looking three stories up to a large stained-glass skylight.

The room was comfortable and inviting for all its vastness. Overstuffed, chintz-covered couches and chairs were grouped invitingly in small conversational clusters that focused on either the large fireplace or the etched French doors that led to the wraparound porch.

"Michael, it's just enchanting," Callie complimented.

"So are you." He was leaning against the door watching her, noting her terrific legs beneath the flare of her skirt and how her breasts pressed against the fabric of her swimsuit. He felt a familiar tightening in his loins. Lately it happened whenever she was in the same room. "Let me take that for you," he said, motioning toward the bright yellow bag she had slung over one shoulder. In two steps he was next to her, tossing the bag onto the nearest chair and pulling her into his arms.

"I've waited all day for this," he said before his mouth descended to hers for a kiss that made her cling even more tightly to him.

It was several minutes before they pulled themselves apart. Michael led her to one of the large couches near the French doors and there, in the fading light of day, they lost themselves in each other's arms. Sighs and moans of pleasure were the only sounds as they took turns getting to know one another in a way only touching could satisfy.

Though he caressed her everywhere, Michael made no move to undress her. Between their long drugging kisses he seemed content to stroke her arms and legs and follow the curves of her back and hips. Several times when his mouth left hers he allowed his lips to trail lightly down her neck, following the V of her swimsuit to her breasts, but he always returned to further explore her mouth.

Callie was becoming senseless from wanting more from him. She caught fistfuls of his hair and almost angrily pulled him to her, arching her neck and back and inviting his most intimate explorations.

Instead of accepting her invitation, though, he pulled himself free and stood up, holding one hand out to her. "Let's go for a swim, Callie."

She looked at him incredulously. She would drown if she tried to swim now; she could barely walk. But she followed him out of the now-dark room through the hall and into a garden surrounding a beautiful free-shaped pool. Flickering torches balanced on the ends of sturdy bamboo stakes lit the area around the pool. The night was completely dark and almost silent.

"Come on," he urged, letting go of her hand and diving into the aqua water. He swam to the center of the pool and held out his arms to her. Callie dropped her wrap skirt on the edge of the pool and followed him into the water. When she surfaced in front of him, she saw that he had removed his trunks and they were floating toward the edge.

He reached for the strap of her suit, and with a motion so sensuous she shivered he eased down each strap until her full throbbing breasts were exposed. When she made no move to stop him but simply looked at him with gray eyes brimming with desire, he dived underwater. In an instant her tiny black suit floated to the surface and away.

Floating together in the silent green world, they were like two of the dolphins who often played near the lighthouse—floating and touching and then surfacing in a flash before submerging themselves again. They were both excellent swimmers, and were soon frolicking and chasing each other through the warm water.

There was something about the almost primitive setting that left them with no inhibitions. Again and again they found themselves tangled together like seaweed, falling together to the bottom of the pool as they kissed passionately and then exploding to the surface for a long gulp of air before locking themselves together again.

Callie clung to him, pulling his face toward her breast as she teased his ear with her tongue. She knew by now that this could drive him wild and his reaction would be almost savage in its desire.

"Callie," he groaned, then pulled her against him.

She felt the need he had for her and she adjusted her body to fit with his and wrapped her legs around him. He carried her out of the pool and into the white latticed gazebo where the firelight played through the pattern of the framework to reveal a double chaise lounge.

"Callie? Are you sure this is what you want?"

"Very much, Michael. Maybe you're the one who isn't sure?" He seemed so hesitant as he lay beside her stroking her wet body and combing his fingers through her hair.

He laughed and rolled on top of her pinning her firmly to their wicker bed. "Are you serious? Don't you know that I practically had to be handcuffed to keep from bringing you to my bed before this? Holy criminy, lady, if we'd danced one more time at the Duck, I was ready to take you right there on the floor. I've never wanted a woman as much as I want you, Callie, but I knew for you and I it had to be more than just a mere tumble into bed." This last came in a husky whisper just before his lips descended on hers, and she felt his knee urging her legs to part and let him in.

"Tell me what you like, Callie," he whispered. "Slow down, we've got all night. Do you like this?" Callie felt pressure points she didn't know she had. "Or this." He rolled over until she was on top of him and he was touching her everywhere with his hands and mouth and body.

For a long time they experimented with each other and gave one another the reward of cries of pleasure and moans of passion until Callie began to feel a sensation building within her she'd never felt before. She held on to Michael very tightly as the raging tide threatened to engulf and carry her away. She knew if she gave in to it she'd be totally out of control. Callie had never allowed herself to be out of control—ever. But the feelings Michael stirred in her urged and demanded that release and Callie found holding on impossible.

"Callie, don't be afraid. Let it come." He watched her struggle with her emotions. At that moment, his own control was at the breaking point, but he was determined to wait for her to make her own decision. He felt her nails rake his shoulders as she balanced herself above him. The moisture on their skin was no longer water from the pool. He waited, stroking, coaxing, and watching for any sign that she had decided to give in to the feelings that were so clear in her eyes.

Callie heard Michael's gentle coaxing and the sounds of the night around them. She felt the sum-

mer breeze surround them and caress the two of them.
She smelled the pool and the night air and the garden, but she was most aware of the taste and scent and
feel of Michael beneath her. His skin was incredibly
smooth, while his muscles were powerful and tense,
working to give her pleasure.

"Michael." She stroked his face until he opened his
eyes to her. He turned with her then, breathed her
name and then cried it out as together they released
their desire.

Finally surfacing for air, they smiled delightedly at
each other. They lay together naked and silent listening to the sounds of a summer Florida night on the
bay. They'd barely spoken to each other since her ar-
rival hours earlier. Their bodies had spoken vol-
umes, though, and words seemed not only
unnecessary but an intrusion.

"You must be starved," he whispered as he began a
new examination of her ear with his lips.

"No," she replied, surprised. Ordinarily she would
have been ravenous, but tonight she just wanted to be
here next to him.

"I'm not hungry, either—" he grinned and pulled
her to her feet "—not for food anyway." He led her
back to the pool, and together they slipped into the
warm water.

"Woman, I'm obsessed by you," he murmured and
pulled her to the shallows where they could both
stand. He lifted her until he could enter her while she

wrapped her legs securely around his waist and hips. This time there was no need for him to wait for her to make up her mind to join him. She matched his passion until together they again found the crest. This time instinctively Callie rode it joyously until she was left relaxed and spent in the arms of her lover.

They stayed like that—in each other's arms against the edge of the pool—for a long time before climbing out and walking back to the gazebo. They slept on the double chaise wrapped together in the warm night with a curtain of mosquito netting for protection.

Twice more they turned to each other in the night and made slow, languorous love. Only their exhaustion could dampen their desire.

"YOU MUST BE HUNGRY by now."

Callie opened one eye to see Michael through the haze of the netting. Dressed in faded jeans, shirtless and barefoot, he was carrying a tray filled with coffee, juice, and muffins.

"Hi," she murmured sleepily and pushed aside the cotton blanket he'd evidently covered her with sometime after dawn. Her stomach growled and he laughed.

"Here, eat." He handed her a hot muffin and a glass of juice while he set the tray on a table and poured the coffee.

Suddenly Callie felt shy and tried to hold the blanket over her breasts while she devoured the food. He turned to hand her the coffee and saw her embarrassment. Instead of teasing her out of it, he sat down heavily on the edge of the lounge, his eyes clouding.

"That's probably a good idea—covering up." He nodded toward the clutched coverlet. "After last night..." He got up and stalked around the gazebo, and as he paced he pulled his fingers through his unruly, sun-drenched hair. Callie nibbled her muffin and watched him.

"Michael?" She put the coffee cup back on the tray and stood up, reaching for him.

"Callie, it's never happened that way before. I couldn't get enough of you. Move in, Callie. Here, with me, today... this morning."

"What?" She couldn't believe she was hearing him right.

"I'm telling you I am obsessed by you. I can't work or sleep. I need you with me—all the time. Dammit, I think I'm in love with you."

"After one night?" But it was more than just one night and they both knew it. She was afraid to admit her own feelings that had developed over the past weeks. Nothing—not even her crusade for preserving the island—had been able to stem the surge of the growing passion she had for this man. Whether she would name that feeling love, Callie didn't know. But she was sure that they were a long way from being free of one another.

"That was no ordinary night of lovemaking and we both know that. Most people don't get that in a lifetime, Callie. It was more than sex—at least for me. You don't get that kind of an explosion by simply mixing two bodies. What we shared last night has to do with what we've been sharing for weeks—communication on every level."

He had come to stand directly in front of her, and while he didn't touch her, his eyes challenged her to deny his power to ravage her with a single look. "Move in, Callie." To her it sounded almost like a command.

"Why?" she demanded in return.

"Why?" Momentarily he was speechless. "Why? Because I need you here. Because we're two very busy adults who don't have to play teenage dating games as a prelude to making love."

"Oh, then it's a purely practical decision—not very romantic, but terribly efficient?" Her sweet smile belied the tension she held in check.

A phone Callie hadn't noticed rang, startling both of them. For several rings Michael didn't answer. Then with an oath he practically ripped it off the wall.

"Brookstone," he stated, and then listened for several minutes. "When?" His voice was clipped, his posture tense. "How?" He tapped the wall of the gazebo with one fist. "Did you get to the families?" He sat heavily on the lounge, and his voice was flat and tired. "I'll be there this afternoon. Have Arnold meet me . . . with some answers." He hung up then and for several minutes he sat with his head in his hands.

"Is there anything I can do?" she asked finally.

"A construction site in Chicago—the whole thing collapsed this morning just as the crews arrived. Two guys are dead, maybe more. I've got to get up there."

"Do they know what caused it?"

"I don't know yet. Something tells me there was a screwup on the substructure. I told Arnold that bastard couldn't be trusted—he's been in some scrapes before, but Arnold wanted to give him a chance. Now two women just had to be told their husbands won't be home for dinner. Damn. . . ." He paced the room like a caged animal.

"What can I do?" Callie asked again, beginning to dress and straighten their bed.

"Just be here when I get back," he said, watching her as she performed the mundane housekeeping chores. "Leave that, Callie, and come here." He caught her in his arms and forced her to meet his eyes. "Will you be here when I get back?"

"I'll be here, Michael, but I won't be living here. Not yet."

"I guess that'll have to do for now. Will you drive me to the airport?"

"Of course." She finished dressing, noting that he had brought her bag and clothing out to the gazebo for her. Together they walked around the pool and back toward the house.

"Callie?" He caught her arm and held her before opening the back door. "I know it's sudden, but I'll do whatever it takes to get you to admit that we belong together."

"You sound very sure of yourself, Michael Brookstone," she said, trying to coax a smile from him.

He grinned for the first time since the phone call. "You want romance? Terrific," he answered his own question. "Because, lady, I'm going to be the most romantic guy you ever met. Get ready, Callie Barnes, to be swept off your beautiful sexy feet."

7

BECAUSE SHE WAS NEEDED at the paper, Callie had dropped Michael at the door of the airport in Fort Myers and returned to Sanibel. As she pulled into her reserved spot at the *Press* she noticed a local florist's truck pulling away. She hoped they'd been there to drop off the copy for their new ad; she'd been waiting for it for three days.

"Hi, Jer. What's up? Florist leave the copy?" She pushed her sunglasses onto the top of her head and poured herself a cup of coffee.

"Yep, and a little something else." He nodded toward her desk. "How the hell can you drink coffee when it's ninety degrees?"

But she didn't answer. On her desk was a large orchid plant in full bloom. It was breathtaking. The card said simply, "Michael."

"Careful, little girl. It's a small island." Jerry was watching her over the tops of his bifocals as she read the card.

"What's that supposed to mean?"

"It means I tried to reach you all last night and *very* early this morning and you weren't home. And it means a tip came in this morning that Brookstone may lose his shirt in Chicago because of a faulty substructure, and he's gone up there to see what he can salvage." Jerry ripped a page out of his typewriter and passed it to her. It was the beginning of the story on the benefit with comments about the problems in Chicago. "Now I wonder why all of this comes as no surprise to my publisher."

Callie turned away from him. It had been a long morning already. "My private life has nothing to do with this," she mumbled.

"Then you're a dreamer because this is the big league, and you can bet this paper that every contractor who wants to get his hands on one of those precious permits will cry foul the minute they hear about you and Brookstone. The council is old-fashioned, Callie, and they won't stand for anything that smacks of favoritism. Either you give up Brookstone or you give up the crusade—you can't have both."

"We'll see about that," Callie said tersely, and pulled her chair up to her desk to edit the story on the lighthouse.

MICHAEL HAD BEEN GONE for two weeks when Callie decided to take a walk down to the lighthouse and check on the progress there. Every night Michael called, and they talked for hours. She told him Jerry was pushing her to do a story on the Chicago scandal and Michael agreed she should. "And, Callie? Tell it from both sides. Maybe you should come up here yourself and get the full scoop," he suggested hopefully.

"You know I can't," she said sadly, and told him of all the things she was trying to do to get ready for the coming tourist season. She also relayed Jerry's comments about their relationship, branding the whole idea as ridiculous. But Michael agreed with Jerry. "He's got a good point," he said. "We both need to be very careful to protect our reputations now."

After that call, Michael sent her gifts and flowers every day, but they arrived from shops off the island, never from local merchants. His latest gift came from a fashionable boutique in Chicago and had been air-expressed to her door.

Inside was a very small one-piece swimsuit that looked as if it was made of snakeskin. When she tried it on she found that it was high cut on each thigh and deep in the neckline, leaving practically nothing to the imagination.

"Michael," she chastised him when he called, "this is almost obscene and it's most certainly indecent. I can't wear this."

His sexy chuckle sent a shiver up her spine. "It's perfect, then. And I have just the place for you to wear it as soon as I get back there."

"When will that be?" Callie had missed him more than she would have thought possible, nightly reliving their lovemaking.

"I just don't know. I'm shooting for next week, but honestly, the attorneys are going crazy, not to mention the insurance people. And Arnold is a basket case; the death of these two guys has really torn him apart." He paused. "It's been pretty rough. Callie? Come up here."

"You know I can't," she said. "The paper..."

"Damn the paper." As though he could sense her tensing, he quickly went on. "Okay, calm down. I didn't mean that, but Lord I miss you." He laughed softly then. "The city of Chicago is going to triple my water bill if I take many more cold showers, lady."

"You shouldn't send all these presents, Michael."

"Don't change the subject. And why not? I'm courting you. Unfortunately, I'm doing it long distance so I have to try harder. Wait till you see what's coming tomorrow."

"Michael," she wailed, and he laughed.

"What's happening down at the lighthouse?" He'd asked her to keep an eye on the project, but she'd been so busy with the paper and the preservation committee that it had been several days since she'd been down there. "Do me a favor and get down there tomorrow? Marlena says things are happening pretty fast. I have to go.... I love you." He waited a beat, but she didn't echo his words. "Good night, Callie."

"Good night," she answered, and hung up the phone. "I love you, too," she whispered, her hand still on the receiver.

The next morning she was awakened early by a delivery man bearing two pounds of fresh jumbo shrimp. The gift was accompanied by a note with an invitation to dinner at Michael's Chicago penthouse. The note also promised that a driver would pick her up at two o'clock. This courtship was costing him a fortune. She decided it couldn't hurt to spend a day or two in Chicago, after all he'd been through.

Callie called Marlena to check on the arrangements, and by midmorning she was on her way to the lighthouse. The day was very hot and still—the island fairly simmered.

There were no workmen around as she picked her way through the bulldozers and other heavy equipment abandoned for the weekend around the building site. She followed the lines of the plans she'd practically memorized and found herself face-to-face with a huge cypress tree that had always marked one of her favorite daydreaming spots on the island.

Callie rewalked the plan, making sure of her steps, and found herself again directly in the path of the tree. More to the point, the old tree was in the path of the foundation. Something would have to give, and Callie was sure it would be the tree. She paced the area for several minutes, trying to see how the destruction of the landmark could be avoided, but she could see no way to keep it from being cut down. "Damn," she muttered and headed for home.

THE BROOKSTONE JET was a flying home. It had seating room for ten and full living quarters, including a bedroom, complete bath with shower, large-screen television. There was a crew of three to fly the plane and serve the passengers. Since Callie was the only passenger she was mostly alone in the luxurious cabin. Had she not been fastening a seat belt, she thought, it would have seemed as if she was in some elegant living room.

Once they were in flight the steward brought her coffee and a light lunch and told her what their flying time to Chicago would be. He offered her a choice of films to watch. When she declined that entertainment he pressed a button and one panel silently opened to reveal an extensive library of books and magazines, plus the daily papers from several major cities around the country. Callie gulped, flashed the steward a smile, and selected a paper.

When they touched down in Chicago the pilot phoned to inform her that the weather in Chicago was eighty degrees and raining. The Brookstones' limousine, he said, would pull up next to the stairs of the plane and take her into the city. Callie thanked him and put the phone away. She checked her hair and makeup in the bathroom, then took her seat and waited while the plane taxied up to the hangar.

The steward, solemn and unobtrusive as always, had provided her with a bright yellow rain slicker and umbrella. Through the window she could see the chauffeur transferring her single suitcase to the trunk of an enormous black car.

It rained hard all the way into the city and Callie could feel her hair curling around her face. She tried unsuccessfully to flatten it into a more sedate style but finally gave up and allowed it to wave around her cheeks and ears.

The driver traveled along familiar Michigan Avenue until he was nearly at the Water Tower Place and then turned onto a side street a few blocks from the lake. Callie recognized the building where they stopped as one she and Sonny had once dreamed of owning an apartment in. At the time, even though Sonny had been earning a substantial income, they hadn't been able to afford this particular address.

The doorman ushered her through a paneled lobby to the Brookstones' private elevator. Until the night he had unveiled his plans for the lighthouse she'd had no idea that Michael came from this much money; she definitely felt out of her league in these posh surroundings.

The minute the doors to the elevator slid open, Callie was met by a uniformed maid who took her coat and stepped aside to allow her to enter the penthouse's living room. The chauffeur waited discreetly by the door with her luggage.

"Take Ms Barnes's things to her room, Dorothy, and then you and the others take the rest of the weekend off." Michael stood by the French doors that led to the rooftop pool and garden.

"Thank you, sir," Dorothy replied with a smile and disappeared down a long hallway.

"Callie, oh Callie." In long strides Michael crossed the room and swept her into his arms, swinging her around and around. When he stopped he held her and kissed her hungrily, his hands caressing her back and shoulders.

"Michael," she said, taking a step away and trying to straighten her clothes in case Dorothy or one of the other servants he'd alluded to came into the room.

"Come back here," he grumbled, and once again pulled her into his powerful embrace. "I can't believe you're here," he whispered against her hair, which was still damp from the rainstorm. "You smell like summer showers."

"Maybe that's because I just got drenched by one," she said, laughing. Then she became serious. "I have to be back Monday morning, Michael."

"But I want to show you Chicago. More to the point, I want to show Chicago you."

"I used to live here, Michael. Remember?"

"But you told me everybody saw only Sonny," he teased.

"That's no joke, Michael." She tried to sound stern, but he felt so good next to her, that all she could do was sigh and snuggle closer. "Monday," she repeated firmly as if trying to convince herself.

"We'll fly back together tomorrow night, then. I decided I had to get back myself, before I lose everything on Sanibel, too." His arm encircled her waist, and they walked together into the spacious living room. "What do you think?" he said, making a sweeping gesture to encompass their surroundings.

"It's very..." Callie searched for a word that could politely describe the austere, modern room.

"Impersonal? Unfriendly? Cold?" Michael provided, with a tinge of bitterness.

"Well, sometimes decorators get carried away with a theme, Michael. They create magazine portraits and forget families live in the rooms."

"Then what they did here was perfect—I wouldn't exactly call the Brookstones a family in the cozy sense of the word."

"But surely your parents love each other, Michael. They've been married a long time, and there's little doubt they love you. Why would they back the lighthouse project if they didn't?"

"My parents have a marriage of convenience, Callie. Two old fortunes making a merger. Mother provided the obligatory heir—*moi*—and that was that. I was raised by the likes of Dorothy and the chauffeurs and spent my childhood in boarding and military schools." He sat on one of the only comfortable pieces of furniture in the room and pulled her down beside him. "I didn't think you'd come," he said as he nibbled her ear.

"I almost didn't," she said, then told him about her visit to the lighthouse and the old cypress tree.

"So I'm about to destroy one of your precious trees and you came anyway? Now that's progress." He leaned close until their foreheads were touching.

"Well, there didn't seem to be anything I could do about the cypress. It's my own fault. If I'd gone down there even a couple of days ago I might have been able to save it."

"Stay right there." He reached for the phone next to them and dialed a long distance number. Waiting for an answer, he watched her as if she might disappear were he not holding her there with his eyes. "Marlena? Mickey.... Yeah, she's here, thanks...." He laughed, then turned very businesslike.

"Marlena, get in touch with Jeff Moser. Tell him to get his crews and his chopper out to the lighthouse first thing Monday. I want that cypress tree moved.... No, you heard me, moved—not cut down. I don't—Marlena, I don't give a damn about the lumber for the Sinclair house. Appeal to their sense of preservation. Tell them the tree will be there for everyone, not just those guests who happen to wander into their living room and won't give a damn where the wood came from.... No, don't get an estimate, get it done. Okay? ... Yeah. Goodbye." He replaced the receiver and turned back to Callie, who was watching him dumbfounded.

"You're going to move a one-hundred-year-old tree?"

"Sure."

"How?"

"I just hired a crew and a helicopter. They'll lift the tree and move it to a spot where it won't be in the way of the foundation and where it can still be an intricate part of the total design. Jeff's a landscape architect on my staff. He's dynamite—you'll think the tree grew for a hundred years right where he sits it down." Michael was so matter-of-fact about the whole plan Callie found herself almost believing that moving a giant cypress could be as simple as one-two-three.

"We're leaving now, Mr. Brookstone." Dorothy stood discreetly by the front door, her purse and a shopping bag in hand.

"Fine, Dorothy. Have a great weekend."

"Thank you, sir. The others have already left."

"Okay. See you next time I'm in, and thanks," Michael called after her as she disappeared through what Callie assumed was the kitchen door.

"Alone at last," Michael said huskily, and with Callie next to him, he stretched out on the long sofa. He was kissing her hungrily and telling her how happy she had made him by just being there when the phone rang again. He groaned and reached for it. "This is the last call, I promise. Brookstone," he said into the receiver, and listened, becoming more agitated the more he heard. "I didn't want an estimate . . . I told you that.... Marlena, I don't give a damn if it costs ten *million*—do it." He banged the receiver back into place and took Callie back into the circle of his arms.

"Michael," she said softly, her mouth near his ear, "how much is it costing to move the tree?"

"Skip it," he said, obviously distracted by her warm breath.

"How much?" She raised herself on one elbow to look at him.

"Ten thousand, okay? Now can we drop it?"

"Michael!" She started to protest but he stood up and, lifting her in his arms, began to carry her down the long hallway toward the bedrooms. "It's time for you to pick your accommodations and get ready for dinner. Now then we have the blue room . . . the yellow room . . . the rose room," he announced, pushing open each door with his foot until she had seen six or seven rooms.

"Which one is yours?"

He smiled and opened the last door on the hall to reveal a totally masculine lair of leather furnishings, cherrywood walls, brass accents, a fireplace and the largest king-size bed she'd ever seen. Gently he placed her in the center of the bed. "Your robe, m'lady," he said, and ceremoniously draped a dark green satin man's bathrobe across the foot of the four-poster. "Shall I draw a warm bath for you, ma'am? You look quite tuckered after your journey." He didn't wait for a reply, but strode with authority to the adjoining bathroom leaving Callie alone.

She undressed and in the background heard what seemed to be several sprays of water running at the same time. She wrapped the robe tightly around her, but it was far too large and kept dropping off one shoulder as she tried to tie the sash.

"Your bath is ready," Michael called, and she went to the door of the bathroom. When she pushed it open she found herself in a bright room full of plants, with a large window looking out on the Chicago skyline. In the center of the room raised on a platform three steps up was a large whirlpool. Michael sat in the swirling waters and held out his hand to her. "It isn't the pool, but then it's too wet for swimming outside anyway."

Callie smiled and dropped the robe, standing frozen for a moment, disoriented by the multiple reflections of herself in the mirrors that covered the walls. When she heard Michael's sharp intake of breath, she climbed the three stairs and eased herself into the warm foaming water.

Tentatively at first Michael touched her lips with his, hands resting lightly on her shoulders. But then he groaned and pulled her forcefully against him, plundering her mouth with his tongue. Callie relaxed in his embrace, giving in to the private whirlpool she felt inside as her mind and body swirled with desire.

As before, there was something primitive and ageless about their lovemaking. Oblivious to the amount of water they sent splashing down the tile stairs they strove to find a release for the need each of them had held in check for weeks. Quickly they reached the pinnacle of their passion, and each sang pleasure at the other's power to give such satisfaction.

Slowly they relaxed against the side of the tub, and Michael started to soap Callie's entire body. When he was done she washed him, but by the time she was finished there was no playfulness in the act. Each wanted the other again, their appetites clearly reflected by eyes that glazed with sensuality.

"Callie." He murmured her name against her hair.

"Hmm?" Her finger traced a trail through the wet curls that covered his chest.

"I can't do this again." He felt her stiffen; she had misunderstood his meaning. It made him smile. He pulled away so she could see his laughing eyes. "I'm too old to play acrobat in a bathtub more than once a day."

She started to laugh then and together they got out of the tub and dried off. In the bedroom he pulled back the covers and they snuggled together in the bed. "Tell me everything I missed—island gossip, everything," he said as she settled closer in the crook of his arm.

"You first. Are you really all right, Michael?" Callie had noticed a sad weariness in Michael's face the moment she had walked through the door. She held his hand and stroked the lean, callused fingers.

He sighed heavily then, releasing some of the tension he'd held inside during these nightmarish weeks since the collapse of the project. "It's been pretty awful. I never want to have to face someone's family and be the one to tell them their husband and father died because I took the lowest bid. Sometimes I think this empire, or whatever it is, is more responsibility than one man ought to handle. If I had been here—if I had studied the specs personally, if—"

"You can't take all the blame on yourself, Michael. It was a terrible thing, yes, but there were lots of people involved, not just you. You can't take all this on your shoulders."

"It's not just that. I keep going over in my mind what I might have done. I see my men looking at me differently now, with a little less trust. Hell, I look at me with less trust. I can only imagine what Mackin and the others on Sanibel are doing with this."

"Jerry and I have managed to keep it all pretty low key. We've been focusing on the lighthouse project. Of course, the mainland papers have been full of it." She wished she could soften it for him, but she knew he would have seen all the front page stories, complete with pictures and screaming headlines, in newspapers from all over Florida.

"I'm not sure it's such a good idea for the *Press* to downplay this, Callie. You've got to be objective.

How would you have covered it if it had been Mackin or one of the others?"

"But—"

"No buts, Callie. You could be risking the integrity of your paper and indirectly your efforts to save the island." He had raised himself on one elbow and was lecturing her now, his brow deeply furrowed.

"Okay, Mr. Brookstone—" she shoved an imaginary microphone under his nose "—tell me, are any of the same companies you use here in Chicago on the disastrous Roosevelt project involved with the Lighthouse Colony? And what about the substructure there? Can it withstand high winds and decades of pounding water? What happens if a hurricane hits?"

"Hold it." He held up both hands, laughing. "Hold it. No comment, okay? I didn't mean you had to protect your integrity this very moment. I mean, give a man a chance to at least get his pants on, lady."

"Oh, but with his pants off he's much less intimidating and far more interesting," she teased, and started to run her fingers up and down the inside of his thigh.

"Less intimidating, huh? I'll show you how wrong you are, Ms Publisher." In a second he had pinned her to the bed. She struggled, but not very much.

She had missed him, despite the daily phone calls. She had missed his . . . presence. Not just their shared passion, but their discussions of ideas and their bantering and their just being together, without making love or talking. Had she been able to read his mind, she would have found her own thoughts mirrored there.

"I've missed you, Callie," he murmured before covering her mouth with his.

Hours later, Callie lay tangled in a mass of monogrammed linens and pillows. Michael dozed, his head resting on her shoulder, his mouth near enough that she could feel every breath. She watched him sleep as the light faded and night fell.

Thinking about what he had said, Callie knew he was right. It was becoming harder though for her to be objective about Michael or his business. She was so in love with him it was impossible to believe anything bad could be associated with his name or work. Yet she had to do the story without any bias on her part.

Michael stirred and began to tease her nipple with his tongue until it rewarded him by flowering under the tender urging of his mouth. "Callie?"

"Hmmm?" She was thinking about the slant of the story, and there was a frown on her face.

"What about moving in?"

He had said it softly, but she felt his body tense as he waited for her answer. "I can't, Michael."

He sat up then and switched on the small bedside lamp, which cast a golden glow over them as he studied her face. "Why not? Don't you know whether you love me?"

She tried to turn away. "It isn't that."

"It isn't that? Does that mean you love me?" He caught her face and forced her to meet his eyes.

"Yes, Michael, I do. I love you very much."

He smiled then—the same engaging boyish grin she'd first been attracted to on the plane in the spring. "Well now, that's not a bad start."

8

THAT JUNE SUNDAY in Chicago was gray and muggy; Callie felt there was something almost ominous in the air. Michael, however, was like a kid out of school. He woke her at dawn, and together they took a morning run through the still-sleeping streets of the north shore area. Along Michigan Avenue the only eyes that followed them were those of the mannequins in the high-fashion shops that lined the street.

When they reached Tiffany's Michael pulled her to a halt and made her look in the windows for something she liked. Callie examined the rings and diamonds and ropes of pearls and pronounced every piece much too gaudy for Sanibel.

Back at the penthouse they showered and relaxed in the whirlpool, and Callie used the shrimp left from their dinner to whip up seafood omelets for breakfast. The kitchen was as sterile and high tech as the rest of the place. Everything was spotless and in its place, and there was no sign that this kitchen was ever used by breathing, feeling human beings. Callie shuddered slightly as she broke eggs into a gleaming copper bowl.

She served the breakfast on the rooftop next to the pool because other than Michael's bedroom it was the only place she could find that exuded any sense of comfort and welcome.

"What shall we do today?" Michael asked as he leaned back and sipped his second cup of coffee.

"It's your city, you tell me." Callie smiled and relaxed a bit.

"It used to be your city, too," he reminded her. "Why don't we take turns? I'll take you someplace, then you take me. You made breakfast, so I'll take care of lunch."

"Wait a minute, that leaves me stuck with dinner," she jokingly complained.

"Not at all," he protested. "Didn't you islanders ever hear of high tea? You plan that, and I'll do dinner."

"Who's going to do these dishes?" She grinned at him. "After all I made breakfast myself and this isn't some restaurant."

"Okay, you get dressed and I'll do KP."

In an hour they were off, Michael in the lead. He hailed a cab and had them delivered to Grant Park, where they strolled the gardens until the museums opened. They ambled through the Art Institute then, ogling the Monets and Chagalls. From there Callie led the way across the park to the Museum of Natural History, where she could continue her lecture on ecology.

Outside it had started to drizzle and Michael flagged a passing cabbie to take them to Chinatown for lunch. On Wentworth Avenue they felt like they had crossed an ocean rather than the city, for now the sound of Chinese surrounded them and they were the foreigners.

Michael stopped a street vendor and bought each of them a straw coolie hat for protection from the rain. "How do you feel about a walking picnic?" Michael asked as they browsed along the avenue.

"Michael, it's a little wet for a picnic. What's a walking picnic?"

By way of explanation Michael bought them orders of dim sum and popped a piece in Callie's mouth as they continued their walk.

From a produce truck they bought snow peas and from a bakery picked up a bag of overbaked almond cookies at a bargain rate. They were about to get into a cab when Michael suddenly dashed into a shop and emerged moments later with a small box. Callie directed the driver to the Museum of Science and Industry before turning to him.

"Too gaudy?" He opened the box and inside was the most beautiful strand of tiny sea pearls she'd ever seen.

"Michael, they're gorgeous." She turned to allow him to fasten the clasp, then kissed him as the cab sped through the Italian neighborhood and on to the museum.

"This is it, folks, or I could keep driving." The cabbie was watching them in his rearview mirror with a lopsided grin on his craggy face.

Callie and Michael had been locked in an embrace since he'd given her the necklace, completely oblivious to the progress of their ride. Michael smiled slowly at the driver. "Keep driving," he said, and reached for Callie again.

"No," she ordered, laughing. Pulling away, she paid the driver over Michael's protest, and they hurried through the rain to the museum.

Inside they worked their way through the human heart, the coal mine and the German submarine. Callie insisted on seeing the huge dollhouse that once belonged to actress Colleen Moore, and Michael demanded equal time to fully explore the massive train display. By that time it was late in the afternoon and Michael announced he couldn't possibly walk another step. "Teatime," he announced.

Outside, Callie stopped the cab with a whistle through her teeth that caused passersby to turn and stare in appreciation. "I'm impressed," Michael said as he held the car door for her.

They spent a lazy two hours over tea and small sandwiches and fruit at the Ritz Carlton Hotel. "You know," Michael told her, "we could have gone back to the house for this. We're only a couple of blocks away."

"I know," Callie said, and sipped her tea. She didn't want to say that the hotel had more charm than his parents' home.

"It's not exactly the warmest, homiest place in the world, is it?" he said, reading her thoughts.

"It's lovely," she protested. She nibbled a sandwich and then asked, "Did your mother like Bette?"

Michael laughed out loud and leaned back, stretching his long legs toward her. "Not one bit. She was even more furious than Dad when I announced our engagement. At least when Bette started to get some critical acclaim Dad came around. Mother always thought of her as 'that chorus girl.' My mother is not the most subtle person in the world."

"Wonder what she'd think of me," Callie ventured, looking everywhere but at Michael's face.

"Wait a minute. Is my family being rich the reason you won't live with me?"

"Partly," Callie admitted. "Your parents would take one look at my bank balance and be sure I was trying to trap you."

"So what? I'll tell them you're an ecology nut and adamantly against trapping defenseless animals. What's the rest of the reason?"

She studied him for a moment before going on. "We have to get past this mess in our business lives before we can think of a personal life, Michael. I don't like people gossiping about me or my private life. I had

enough of that before, and I won't be involved in a relationship on those terms again."

His jaw tightened, and she saw that stubborn glint
that came to his eye whenever things were not going
his way. "Our private life is just that, Callie—private."

"You know better," she answered gently. "We are
two public personalities in a very small fishbowl. We
have established our businesses to stand for certain
values. We are those businesses, and what we do is far
from private."

"What if we planned to be married...some-
time...?"

Callie heard his hesitation and decided his mention of marriage was either out of desperation or because he thought she would expect it. "I wish it were
that simple, but I know better. Sonny and I—"

"How many times will I have to tell you? I am not
Sonny," he said through gritted teeth.

"I know that. Believe me, Michael, I know that. But
I have to make you see that Sonny and I thought the
gossip couldn't hurt. Reality is that it's a powerful
cancer and it spreads."

"So you are saying no to living with me?"

"For now, I am. Now what's next on our tour?"

He looked at his watch and dashed around to pull
her chair out. "Hurry up, we're late," he urged, practically dragging her through the lobby to the street.
Up the block, they stopped at a movie theater that was

advertising a Charlie Chaplin festival. He bought tickets and hustled her through the doors and up to the small empty balcony.

After the films they took a long leisurely walk up the avenue, window shopping for each other. Michael teased her about how Captain Jack and Ellie might react if she showed up at an island function in one exotic creation they saw in Neiman-Marcus, and she threatened to outfit him in the tight leather pants and jackets featured at Saks.

"Ready for dinner?" he asked when they had walked as far as the Wrigley Building.

"This is ridiculous," Callie said with a chuckle, "we've done nothing but eat all day it seems but, yes, I'm ready to eat again."

"We've also done a lot of walking to burn up all that food, and we really haven't eaten so much." He saw her raise one skeptical eyebrow and laughed. "Anyway I told you, you're much too skinny." He poked her in the ribs.

By the time they had eaten, picked up their luggage and been driven to the airport it was past ten o'clock. It would be late by the time they reached Fort Myers, even later before Callie reached her own house and bed. She was exhausted just thinking about it; the idea of having to be on the job the following morning made her groan aloud.

"Reality beginning to set in?" Michael asked as they fastened their seat belts for takeoff. She nodded and allowed her head to rest on his shoulder as they raced down the long runway and lifted into the black sky. The cabin was barely lit, and the lights of Chicago twinkled below them for several minutes like a million stars.

The phone rang and Michael picked it up at once. He listened while undoing his seat belt and moving around the cabin. "Thanks. Yeah, fine. Call me when we're twenty minutes out." Hanging up, he reached over and turned on a tape. "Care to dance?"

Slowly they moved through the spacious cabin in rhythm with the soft music. Callie leaned against Michael, her arms around his neck. She toyed with his hair and blew soft kisses into his ear, loving the response she aroused in him. His hands moved seductively up and down her spine, massaging her back and caressing her shoulders and neck.

"Tired?" he murmured next to her ear.

"A little," she admitted. "Pleasantly tired though."

He smiled and pulled her down onto the plush seat. He held her there, her head nestled against his chest.

"I think I could fall asleep," she whispered.

"I don't think so—at least not yet." Michael was not smiling as his hands found the opening of her dress and his mouth searched hungrily for hers.

DURING THE NEXT WEEKS Callie and Michael worked, separately and together, stealing time when they could to walk the beaches or share lunches and suppers.

Michael kept up a constant barrage of reasons why Callie should move in with him or at least let him stay at the cottage with her. She rejected each one. The meeting to decide the awarding of the building permits was only days away and they were already too often seen together at restaurants and island functions. Callie hoped the days of gossip and speculation were behind them, but she wasn't sure. The first stage of the lighthouse project was scheduled for dedication at the end of the month, the interest in the Chicago accident had subsided. Callie had just relaxed into a routine of work and loving Michael when she had an unexpected visitor at the office.

"Someone to see you," Jerry muttered one morning.

Al Mackin bit down hard on his cigar and extended a moist hand for her to shake. "How're you doing, little lady?"

"Mr. Mackin." Callie accepted his handshake. "What can I do for you?"

"Well now for starters how about calling me Al? After all, you're on a first-name basis with certain other developers here on Sanibel, aren't you? Mind if I have a seat?" He settled his bulky frame into the chair across from her desk without waiting for a reply.

Callie decided to ignore his reference to Michael. "Is there something in particular you want, Al?" She said his name with some sarcasm. "And you can call me Callie," she finished sweetly.

"Well, now you know the meeting's coming up Friday." There was no explanation necessary for "the meeting." The entire two islands could talk of little except how the council would be awarding final permits for building any housing up until the year 2000. Its importance could hardly be underestimated.

"And?" Callie prompted.

"Well, now it may be a bit too late for this, but I've been reading your paper here and just about every week there's this big article about Brookstone and his lighthouse thing and hardly a mention about the rest of us developers. Now I'm wondering if that's being real fair, lit—uh, Callie."

"We cover the news, Al. The lighthouse project has been of considerable interest to our readers. Did you have something I should know about for a story?"

"I just thought you might want to reconsider. You've worked real hard to make this paper into the hard-news agency it was when your dad was in charge. But you've lost your perspective on this development thing. You see your daddy would have given equal space to every developer, not tried to sway the council in favor of one certain party." He rushed on before Callie could form the words that were sputtering at her lips. "You see, little lady, your daddy never forgot one thing—" he got up, collecting the cigar he had left balanced on the edge of her desk "—your daddy never mixed business with his pleasures." He nodded to Jerry and left while Callie was still struggling to get to her feet.

"Of all the... Damn that man.... Well..." She whirled around to find Jerry engrossed in a folder of notes on the dedication celebration story. "Jerry?"

Her editor glanced up and then back to his notes.

"Well?" she demanded.

"You really want to hear it?" he asked without looking at her.

She was dumbfounded. "You think he's right?"

Jerry put down the folder and leaned back in his swivel chair. "I think he has a point—a point I believe I made several weeks ago."

"But you're not going to say I told you so?"

"Nope, little lady, you just did. I've got to get a story out. See you later."

"Is everybody going to have a great exit line today?" she shouted to the closing door. The phone rang and its jangle further irritated her. "*Press*," she announced testily.

"Wow." Michael's bass tones came across the wires. "Who burst your balloon?"

"It just isn't my day—everyone else is getting all the best lines."

"What?" He sounded completely confused.

"Skip it. What can I do for you today?" His laugh sounded like a leer, which further irritated her. "Besides that."

"Whoa. Truce. I called to see if we could go to dinner Friday."

"Before the council meeting? I don't know, Michael. That may be a bad idea. I want to cover the story for the paper myself."

"You might have a point."

It wasn't like Michael to give up so easily, and Callie was a little disappointed. "Okay, then I'll see you there," she said gloomily.

"Hold it. What do you think it would look like if we had dinner after the meeting?"

Callie smiled and it carried all the way to her voice. "It would probably look like we were celebrating, and that would be absolutely right."

Michael's voice turned serious for a moment. "If I get those permits, Callie, I owe part of that to you. The competition is good—very good. Your coverage of the project has been important for me, especially after Chicago. See you Friday."

By the time Friday arrived, Callie had begun to think about how well timed the dedication ceremony was; to give Michael's company maximum exposure before the all-important vote. The idea that he might have planned things to work out that way bothered her a bit, but she brushed such thoughts away impatiently.

The council meeting hall was packed with spectators waiting for the vote. Every developer was there with scale models and proposals and staff members and attorneys. Callie took her seat with the other reporters.

The chairwoman called the meeting to order and the room settled into silence. She presented the agenda for the evening, leaving the awarding of the permits as the last bit of business and warning the assembled developers, attorneys and reporters that the meeting would be quiet and orderly or she would have the room cleared.

For the next hour they all sat through the tedious details of minutes, old business, committee reports and finally the report on the permits was called.

The chairwoman announced that each developer would be allowed fifteen minutes to present his proposal and request his permits. At the close of the presentations the council members would be given an opportunity to ask questions and each opposing developer would be given the opportunity to make a brief statement about the proposals of his fellow developers. Then the council would vote, having first received the report of the committee.

There were five companies represented in the room. Michael was the second to make his requests and as the largest developer on the island requested permits for eight projects to be completed by the year 2000. Al Mackin leaned back in his chair, smoking the ever-present cigar and watching his young rival.

Mackin, who had been a developer of island property longer than the others, had only recently returned to the building of housing units after several years working in shopping complexes and offices for the thriving island business community. Until now he and Brookstone had not really been after the same permits, and Brookstone's long success story with condos and time-share units gave him a decided edge. Mackin presented his plans and also requested eight of the precious permits.

It took nearly two hours for the developers to make their presentations and hear the questions raised by the council members. By the time they got around to final statements, the chairwoman urged five-minute limits and made a ceremony of placing her wrist-watch by her place, stating her intention to enforce the rule. Everyone leaned forward to hear the summations.

Michael was eloquent as he pointed out that each of his projects was designed to enhance not only the present but dignify the history of the island while preserving that flavor for the future. He modestly referred to the company track record but refrained from reminding the council of his generous donation of the lighthouse project to the island.

The other developers, with the exception of Mackin, were seeking only two or three permits each and pointed to their own track records in building on other parts of the Florida coastline. Mackin was the last to speak. He came to the podium and balanced his cigar neatly on the edge of the wood surface. He took his time adjusting the microphone and looked directly at each member of the council before speaking.

"Well, we're all on the same side here now, aren't we? And we're hearing a lot about track records tonight. But let's be honest, getting one of these permits is a little like a run for the presidency—it's a political race pure and simple. I'm here to say that Mr. Brookstone over there has run one hell of a race—pardon me, ladies."

Callie couldn't believe this man. He was using every trick in the book to come across as the old Southern gentleman, the friendly guy down the block, when in fact he had never even lived on the island. She looked up at Michael and was astonished to see a slight smile on his handsome face.

"Of course, these other young fellows have been right in there, too," Mackin continued, "but Brookstone—well, that boy's a real master now. You other fellows ought to take some notes here. He's got that lighthouse thing going, which he didn't bother to mention. Of course, he doesn't really need to since at least one paper in town has been filled with stories about the generous Mr. Brookstone."

"Mr. Mackin," the chairwoman said, glancing at her watch, "you have about a minute."

"Right. All I want to say is this. We're all honest folks here with the same interests, the same plans and hopes. When you ladies and gents give out those permits tonight let's just don't be influenced by any grand gestures on the part of certain developers. And let's don't let ourselves be swayed by what the local media might have to say about us. This is a small town where the media's life is as much news as the developer's. Okay, Harriet, I'm done."

Callie was livid, waiting impatiently for Michael to do something—she didn't know what. She had been positive Michael would be up and on his feet in protest at this man's effrontery. But looking around the room she saw that people were shifting restlessly in their chairs while members of the council pored over their notes. To her utter amazement she noticed Michael lean toward Al Mackin and say something that had the older man smiling.

When the dust had settled Michael had been awarded all eight of his permits, Mackin had six and the others divided four. The final permits the council had decided to hold for the time being. Following the announcement the chairwoman adjourned the meeting and the hall was filled with the sounds of scraping chair legs and shouts of congratulations.

Callie headed for the door and her car to wait for Michael. When he arrived a few minutes later, he was beaming. "How about that?"

"Yes, how about that?" Callie answered, but Michael was so elated he was totally oblivious to her sarcasm.

"Where shall we go to celebrate? How about the Duck—I feel like someplace loud and lively tonight, okay?" He opened the door for her.

Callie was so furious she slammed the door without getting in and whirled to face him. She kept her voice low so as not to be overheard by the others who now filled the small parking lot. "Michael, Al Mackin did . . . Were you asleep or what? The man practically branded me in front of the entire town."

He was still smiling. "That's a little strong, Callie," he said, chuckling, and then sobered at once when he realized she was about to hit him. "You're serious, Callie. The man— That's just...business. He needed an edge; he used what he could get. Nobody took that seriously."

She didn't give an inch. Her eyes were steel gray and locked on his, daring him to tell her how their personal life was fair game in a business war. "Is that the way you do business, Michael?" Her voice was very quiet.

Michael rubbed his hand through his hair and looked at her. He'd been so high—eight permits! "Sometimes," he answered. "It's business, Callie. They use what they can to get an edge. Mackin used what he thought would get to the council. He thought by using the lighthouse and us he might get the council to vote against me and for him on the basis of not wanting to seem to be playing favorites, but it didn't work. We got the permits."

"Was he right about the lighthouse?" Callie was the sharp-eyed reporter all the way now.

Michael half expected to see her flip open her notebook. "Maybe," he answered truthfully. "Maybe a little. The timing was no accident—that was right on target. Why the hell do you think I've been busting my buns since I got back here to get that thing on track?"

"What if you'd been off a week?"

"We almost were. Your damned tree set us back—" At once he was sorry he'd said anything. "Look, Callie, if we'd been behind it would have given Mackin and the others another edge. Brookstone promises but can he deliver? Brookstone is falling behind...he's too ambitious...."

"Maybe that's it," Callie said almost to herself.

"What?" He realized something subtle but important was happening here. They were the only ones left in the lot now. The meeting hall was dark, and only an occasional car passed on the road a few feet away. "What's it, Callie?"

She looked at him for a long time as if she were seeing him for the first time. "You are ambitious, Michael. You want it all. Winning is very important to you, isn't it?"

"Winning's important to everybody, Callie."

"It's not important to me," she whispered.

"Now that's a crock and you know it. You came storming down here to save your island from the big bad likes of me. Look me in the face and tell me that isn't wanting to win."

"I just want things the way they were, Michael."

"Callie, things will never be the way they were. Memories are always muted...better than reality, but you have to deal with what is and what's going to be. Then maybe you can make a difference."

"You loved that in there tonight, didn't you? The competition, the timing, the game plan?" Her eyes got large and liquid as she looked at him now. "You like it when we go somewhere and you're recognized and patted on the back and applauded. That's why you wanted to go to the Duck, isn't it? You didn't want to miss the limelight!"

"Callie, you're raving, you know that? All this because Mackin said everybody knew about us? Well, I've got a bulletin for you, lady, everybody does. Now let's go wherever you like."

"You go. I'm tired." She started to get into her car.

"Wait a minute, Callie, what did you want me to do in there—a Sir Lancelot, or what?"

"I'm not sure. I looked up at that table expecting to see an ally—someone as indignant as I was. Instead I saw a couple of old cronies yukking it up over some stupid business deal. Then you come out of there like nothing happened. All you knew was that you got your precious permits, and you were going to be the fair-haired boy tonight. Isn't that about it?" She didn't give him a chance to answer. "Well, let me tell you something, Michael Brookstone, I was married to Mr. Wonderful for nearly ten years and I hated it. I hated the attention, the lack of privacy and especially the lack of identity unless it was linked to him. I won't have that again—I don't care how much I think I love you." And with that she got into her car and roared away.

9

"JERRY, write this up for page one. Give each developer equal space and coverage and be particularly objective on the eight Brookstone projects." Callie tossed the folder of notes on Jerry's desk and turned at once to the coffee.

"I thought you wanted the dedication of the lighthouse project to be the lead." Jerry pretended to flip through the folder, but she felt him watching her carefully over the tops of his glasses.

"This is more relevant. Besides, we may have...overdone our coverage of the lighthouse project a bit. Let's play it down. Lead it on page one of the second section." She remained standing by the window sipping the hot coffee and looking out but she wasn't seeing the view.

"Must have been a long meeting," Jerry ventured as he rolled a fresh sheet of paper into his typewriter. "You look exhausted."

"Yeah." It was all she said before sitting down at her own desk and starting to work.

The morning raced by. Callie had determined the night before to get back to the business of making her paper the best on the island. She wanted the *Press* to take the lead as watchdog over the various projects and developments. After all, that was why she'd come back. She tried to ignore the images of Michael that swam before her eyes.

At eleven a florist truck arrived with a single orchid and a note signed, simply, "Michael." She ignored Jerry's raised eyebrows when she replaced the flower in its box and crushed it into her brimming wastebasket. She pounded out several pages on her typewriter before turning to Jerry.

"Jerry, let me know what you think of this for the editorial." She handed him the pages and turned to greet two reporters who had stopped by for their assignments. When she had sent them off and put a call in to a freelance photographer, she turned to Jerry.

"Well?" She leaned back in her chair and tapped a pencil lightly against her lips.

"It's, uh, pretty strong, Callie."

"I mean for it to be. Can you live with it?"

"I'm not sure," Jerry answered honestly. He reread the pages and Callie waited. What she had written was an impassioned plea for everyone on the island, including journalists, to take a hard look at the future toward which they were headed. She asked for a careful examination of every individual who was in any way responsible for shaping that future. She urged a minute examination of motives as opposed to surface appearances, and she begged for an end to blind acceptance of any individual based on past performance. The allusions to Michael Brookstone were thinly veiled.

"Talk to me, Jerry."

The gray-haired editor took off his glasses and rubbed the bridge of his nose with two fingers. He studied his old friend's daughter. "Callie, I remember you as a young girl running in and out of this office, always with some cause to promote. To you life was always black or white. There was evil and there was good. At ten or fourteen or even twenty it seemed charming. At thirty, I'm not so sure."

"What's that got to do with this?" she asked, motioning toward the editorial.

"I don't think *you* can live with it," he said finally. He picked up the pages and perched his glasses on his perpetually sunburned nose again. "Callie, these references to Brookstone are pretty transparent even if you never mention his name."

"I know," she said stubbornly, and continued to watch him.

"To tell you the truth, Callie, the idea is good. The message is good. But it comes across as some petty lover's quarrel, and you end up looking like some little spoiled kid who's stamping her foot because she can't have her way. Tell me about the meeting and then let me tell you what I think of this."

With a sigh Callie tipped her chair forward and leaned toward him, her slender arms dangling between her legs. "It was pretty awful," she admitted, then related the whole scene to him, from the meeting and Al Mackin's statement to the conversation in the parking lot with Michael. She told him the whole thing with her head bent, studying the tile floor and in a voice that was defeated and low.

"And what would your dad say?" Jerry asked softly.

Callie looked up for a moment and the smallest of smiles touched her wide mouth. "He'd say," and she went into a pretty good imitation of her father's gravelly voice, "Girlie mine, we got two problems here...."

"And you aren't going to solve them both with this." Jerry lifted the editorial and tossed it back on her desk.

"So what do I do?"

"Do you love him?" She nodded. "Then don't try to change him. He is what he is—he's not perfect. A man like Brookstone doesn't get this far without a little ambition, Callie, and despite what you think words like progress and development and profitable are not profanity even here on Sanibel. Think about it." He reached for the ringing phone. "*Press*," he growled, and nodded to Callie. "Brookstone."

"We need to talk."

Michael's voice sounded tired. "Name the place and time."

"Michael, I need a little time to get some things sorted out. I'll see you in a few days—at the dedication." Gently she replaced the receiver and returned to her work.

"You okay, Callie?"

She looked up at Jerry. "I will be. Could you handle the editorial for this week? I think I'd like to rework this." When he nodded she smiled and bent over the words she'd been so sure about earlier.

The day of the dedication was hot and humid even at sunrise when Callie took to the beach for her daily run. She headed for the lighthouse, wanting privacy to explore the work before the ceremonies began later in the morning. The sun was just rising, and there were not many people on the beach.

As she ran she looked at the buildings along the way. She found herself thinking how easily the condo projects fit in next to the smaller older cottages. For the first time neither seemed threatened by the other— they were simply co-existing. In these past months on the island she'd had quite an education in what had been happening here since she'd left for college.

Now she had a new respect for the tourists. She had come to understand that they visited Sanibel because they knew what the island was about; they knew it wasn't about amusement parks and franchises. They knew it was a community of contrasts—Indians and pirates, condos and cottages. More than once she'd been surprised when her reporters had done spontaneous interviews and found the tourists to be aware of the ecological problems, and enthusiastic about playing a part in their solution.

For the upcoming tourist season she had persuaded every motel, cottage and time-share business on the island to display attractive posters that gave information on the ecology of the island and the preservation of the shells, plants and wildlife. She had been pleasantly surprised at the cooperation she'd received from the owners and developers.

Reaching the lighthouse, she climbed carefully around the tree roots that jutted out into the surf before following the beach around to the station. It had been only a few days since she'd been here and she was amazed at how much had been done. Over the weekend the landscaping had been nearly completed, and the site was clear of all debris and machinery.

She had to marvel at Michael's skill in maintaining the flavor of island history while building a place that was durable and secure and efficient.

The lighthouse, true to Michael's word, had been rebuilt in perfect detail, with the exception of an elevator and an observation deck. At the base was a large bronze plate detailing the history of the island and the lighthouse in particular. Everywhere there were gentle reminders to visitors that Sanibel had a special past that would forever flavor its future.

A noise interrupted Callie's solitary thoughts. Startled, she whirled around to see Michael leaning against the giant cypress she'd fought to save. He was watching her, but in the predawn light she couldn't read his expression.

"Hello," she said softly, marveling at how powerful his effect on her always was. "It's really special,

Michael." She waved one hand to include the complex behind her.

He had missed her more the past couple of days than he would have thought possible. The idea that he might have lost her had crossed his mind repeatedly, and the total void he felt when he tried to imagine life without her was devastating. "Have you seen the condos yet?" he asked, still leaning against the tree, studying her.

"No, I didn't think they would be ready."

"The model is. Want to take a look?" He moved toward her slowly, afraid she might make some excuse and leave.

Callie suddenly felt shy and awkward with him. "Sure," she responded in a soft voice, then walked on ahead of him toward the low rambling cottages.

Inside Michael told her to wait by the door. "The power isn't on yet," he explained. Crossing the room, he slid open the glass doors and released the hurricane shutters that covered them. When he opened the shutters and light filtered into the room, Callie gasped, delighted.

The unit was small, but perfect for any artist. First there were multiple sources of light from the sliding glass doors and skylights, as well as sophisticated track lighting. The one large studio room had been attractively divided to allow for a small efficient kitchen and a full, even luxurious, bath and dressing area. It was furnished in welcoming colors of peach and navy, and there was a loft bed with a narrow spiral staircase. Near the windows were the tools of an artist—drafting table, worktable, storage units for supplies, everything.

"In some of the units this area is set up for a writer. For dancers they have mirrors and a barre, the musicians and singers have pianos. . . ." He shrugged and waited.

Callie continued to walk around the studio in awe of its size and feeling of space. When she neared the spiral staircase she raised an eyebrow at Michael and smiled.

Again he shrugged and shoved his hands into the back pockets of his jeans, his open shirt pulling invitingly across his muscled chest and shoulders. "Go on, take a look," he encouraged.

Callie swallowed hard, tearing her eyes away from that body she loved so much, and started up the stairs. At the top she looked at the bed and images of Michael and her making love almost blinded her.

"It's neat," she managed, her voice suddenly husky.

"Try it," Michael urged, and started up the stairs toward her, his eyes devilish.

"Michael, come on. Let me go down." There was no passing him on the stairs.

"Just try it." He grinned, advancing toward her.

"Michael," she said warningly, but her foot caught on the edge of the carpet and she fell backward onto the bed. "Michael!" she cried. "It's a waterbed!" And she was laughing and bouncing when he plopped down beside her.

With a gleam in his eye, he kicked off his loafers and crawled toward her on the bed, deliberately making it pitch and roll so that she was off balance. Callie clung to the railing trying to steady herself, but his playfulness was infectious. He lunged and she tumbled away from him.

They rolled and chased each other until they collapsed in exhaustion across the wildly undulating bed. Callie landed across Michael's legs, her head resting on his thigh.

Michael's eyes were two pools of chocolate when he bent over her. He hesitated for only an instant before he took her mouth under his. If she'd had any doubt of how their separation had affected him, it was erased in that one kiss.

The bed tossed beneath them as he turned her until his powerful body held her captive. His hands found her breasts before moving to the elastic band of her running shorts. His large callused hand slipped under the nylon fabric and covered her taut stomach before moving erotically down to find the dark curls that covered the treasures he sought.

Callie had fought for some control while he kissed her, but as soon as he touched her so intimately all was lost. Her own hands rested briefly in his golden hair, then ran down across the straining cords of his neck to the opening of his shirt.

"Is this shirt a good one?" she asked when he raised his mouth momentarily to tantalize her ear.

"What?" he asked incredulously.

She flipped neatly until she straddled him, holding him captive. "Answer the question," she demanded, settling herself more firmly against the unmistakable rise she felt through his jeans.

"Callie," he moaned, and thrust himself against her.

"Answer," she repeated.

"No, it's nothing. I've had it for years. Callie, what the . . . ?" His eyes widened when she took the opening of his shirt and ripped it completely free causing buttons to fly across the parquet floor below. "I've always wanted to do that," she said simply as she pulled the shirt free of his waistband and lowered herself to take his nipple in her mouth.

"Callie." He moved beneath her, both hands now tucked under her waistband and easing her shorts and panties down her legs. "Woman, you're making me crazy. Let me up so I can get undressed."

She rolled away from him with a grin and finished undressing, then lay back on the wildly tossing mattress to watch him. His body glistened with sweat, for not only was there no electricity, there was no air-conditioning. She liked the way his perspiration highlighted the golden hair that covered his chest and arms and legs.

"Callie," he groaned, "you're making this impossible." He was still trying to get his jeans off, so Callie moved to his feet to pull them free and tossed them on the floor with the rest of their things.

The waterbed cradled and supported them as they made love. Callie welcomed the now familiar build of emotion she'd come to know with him, rejoicing that his rise was as fiery as hers. Together they exploded into a million splintering pieces, then slowly floated back down the rolling sea that was their bed.

"Now can we talk?" Michael pulled one of her damp curls across her face, gently brushing her lips and nose.

Callie smiled but shook her head. "Later," she hedged.

Michael caught the drops of sweat that trickled down her neck with his tongue. "Now," he insisted.

"Later," she said firmly, and kissed him thoroughly.

The sun was high, and the air was now stifling in the studio. "Shall we see if the water works?" Michael said with a grin, raking one hand through his damp hair.

Callie nodded and together they descended the spiral stairs. When they were standing under the cold spray, Michael held Callie close and whispered against her wet hair, "I never want to spend another two days without at least talking to you, lady. And there's only one way I know to guarantee that—marry me."

Callie reached behind him, shut off the spray and started to dry herself. "I can't—not yet," she answered. She wanted to say yes, but she couldn't until she was sure of her own life. The events of the past week had made her uncertain. Oh, she loved him, but was she strong enough not to lean on him when the Al Mackins of the world insulted and challenged her?

"I'm not Sonny," he thundered as he wrapped a towel around his narrow hips and cinched it tightly.

"I know that," Callie replied quietly.

Michael seemed about to say more, then thought better of it and walked into the other room. When she followed him moments later, he had already dressed and gone.

Callie put on her running clothes, then gathered the covers from the bed and the towels in a bundle. She rechecked the unit to make sure there was no sign of disarray and walked slowly up the beach.

No, he wasn't Sonny, she thought. Sonny had been good to her but he had also been very selfish. Sonny had wanted her to make all the sacrifices, forget her career. "What career?" he had once taunted her, and then there had been none.

Now, here on Sanibel, she did have something of her own—the paper, her home, her roots—that belonged to her. They were important to her and if they got in the way of what was important to Michael, which would have to give?

He had asked her that night after the meeting what she had expected of him, and for a time she had thought he was right to think she wanted him up there on his white steed dueling for her honor. But now she knew that wasn't what she had wanted at all. She didn't want a white knight—a rescuer—she wanted a partner. Louise and her father had had that kind of relationship. Suddenly Callie wished she had her mother's support and advice.

She thought of calling West Palm Beach when she reached her house. The morning was waning, though, and she wanted to wash the towels and covers and have them back at the lighthouse.

By the time Callie had done the laundry and driven back to the studio to put everything in place, it was time for the dedication. She rushed home and put on a strapless cotton sundress and flat sandals. Her hair was pulled high off her tanned neck and she used no makeup in an attempt to stay cool during the hot afternoon sun.

Walking to the lighthouse, she decided, would be more convenient than trying to find a parking space in the crowded lot. As she had predicted, the grounds surrounding the complex were teeming with people. Callie saw Michael and started toward him, arriving just as Marlena Davis came at him from the direction of the studios. Marlena was obviously upset.

"Mickey, I'm going to kill those workmen. Do you know they actually used the shower in the model?"

Michael barely controlled a grin. "How can you tell?" He glanced at Callie and smiled openly at her blush.

"The towels, the soap . . . Michael! This is serious!" Marlena was practically stamping her foot.

"Yes, it certainly is. What should we do, Marlena?" But he was looking at Callie.

"I don't know," she moaned. "I found a button on the floor, and there was sand on the stairs leading up to the bed. . . . Oh, my gosh, Mickey, I think somebody actually slept up there."

"Do you now?" Michael was smiling broadly at her. "Well, let's just hope he wasn't alone." At Marlena's wide-eyed surprise and Callie's mortified grimace he took both women by the arm and led them toward the dais. "Shall we?"

The three of them made small talk with various state and local dignitaries for a few minutes, and then Callie heard Ellie's smoky voice at Michael's ear. "Let's get this show rolling, kids. It's too hot to keep these people sitting in the sun for long."

Each local and state politician was introduced for brief remarks. Then each donor to the project was recognized, and a large bronze tablet designed to hang in the lobby of the theater was unveiled in their honor. Callie could see the crowd growing restless with too much pomp and circumstance, and she was nervous for Michael, knowing that being last on the agenda would give him the least enthusiastic audience. He had planned to detail the design for stages two and three of the project, but she doubted there would be anyone left to listen by the time he was introduced.

After what seemed like hours in the scorching sun and searing humidity, Michael finally took the microphone. "I was going to unveil the next phase of the project today but I think we'll let that wait until another time. It's just too hot and I don't know about the rest of you, but it's time for a tall glass of cold anything and a little less formality." With that he shed his navy blazer, loosened his tie and rolled back the sleeves of his white shirt to the applause of everyone.

The crowd dispersed, anxious to look at the shopping center and make their first visit to the observation deck. Several people stopped at the foundation office to make plans for contributing toward support of the project and to join the historical society. Under the giant cypress there was beer and lemonade and platters of fruit and appetizers. Michael was at the center of a lively group. Callie took a lemonade and relaxed against the tree.

Marlena joined her there, commenting, "I see your cypress is doing well."

"Thanks to you, in part. I wish I could have seen that operation."

Marlena shrugged. "Someday you probably can. Michael has things like that done all the time."

They stood in silence for some time observing the festivities. "You must be pleased with today's festivities, Marlena. You've done a wonderful job here."

Throughout the summer Callie had had occasion to observe the other woman at work. She had a great deal of respect for the talent and confidence Marlena brought to her difficult job. There was no question in Callie's mind that Marlena was in this job because she was as intelligent as she was beautiful.

She was interrupted by a light tap on her shoulder and turned to find her mother and Fred smiling at her. "Mom," she shrieked, and hugged Lu tightly in spite of the heat, then it was Fred's turn.

"Why didn't you tell...?" "We wanted to surprise..." "You should have seen your face...." "Oh, I'm so glad...." They all spoke at once.

"Is this a family party, or can an old friend step in?" Michael had joined their circle, unnoticed until he spoke. Then Louise turned with a delighted grin and embraced him while he shook Fred's hand over her shoulder.

"Michael, this is just overwhelming. You must be so proud." Louise sounded as if Michael was her son and she could take full credit for his success.

"Can I show you around?"

"Ellie gave me the twenty-five-cent tour already but Fred hasn't seen it yet. He was too busy visiting when we arrived. Take him, Michael. Callie and I will have a chance to visit. We'll head back to the cottage and start supper, okay?"

Callie was amazed at her mother's ability to direct people with seemingly no intention of taking over their lives. But Callie knew that she was deliberately allowing herself time alone with her daughter and that meant Louise had something to say. Together they watched the men head for the project, and then they walked out to the beach and toward home.

"Well, dear, how is everything?" Louise walked slowly with her head down, occasionally stopping to stoop and examine a shell.

Callie swallowed a smile. "Everything's fine, Mom. How's it going with you?"

Louise shot her a look and wagged one finger at her daughter. "You know what I'm talking about, young lady. Now, talk to me. What's happening with you and Mick . . . Michael?"

"We are seeing each other every day as much as we can. We are working together to try and maintain the work you and Ellie started years ago. We're in love...."

"And?"

"And what?"

"And what are you going to do about that?"

"I didn't think we had to do anything, Mother." Callie gave her parent a look of wide-eyed innocence while she struggled to keep from laughing at Louise's exasperation.

"Callie Barnes, you are deliberately tormenting me. Now come on, when are you getting married? I have plans to make, parties to arrange. I need some notice, you know."

"We aren't." Callie saw her mother's eyebrows shoot up in disbelief and went on, serious now as she tried to explain. "Well, not as in never. It's just that right now..." She struggled to put into words for the first time her own feelings of inadequacy, her fervent desire not to make another mistake, her need to make certain that she wouldn't disappoint Michael and become a burden to him rather than an asset.

"You're making a mistake, Callie," Lu said softly. They walked silently for a time, weaving their way from the water's edge to the hard sand and back again.

Finally Callie asked, "Why? I have to know who I am and be sure of what I can bring to the marriage so that I don't get buried in Michael's shadow the way..."

"The way you did with Sonny? Oh, my darling girl, give yourself some credit for growing, for learning from the past. Doesn't the work you've done here in the past year count for anything in your eyes? On your own, you walked right in and took over a going business and made it better, more profitable than it has ever been before. Do you listen to what people are saying about you? Today at the ceremony, I heard people talking about you—"

"Yeah, I know...gossip and speculation about Michael and me," Callie interrupted.

"You are incredibly insecure in some ways, aren't you?" Louise said with a tinge of disbelief in her voice. "Callie, they were talking about the *Press*, about all the new ideas and interesting stories and projects you've created in such a short time. They were saying how like your father you are—quietly determined to see that Sanibel maintains its history and ecology.

They were saying how Callie *Barnes* has really gotten some people on their toes since she arrived here—not Callie Martoni, not Sonny's ex-wife, nor Michael's new love."

A feeling of pride and self-satisfaction began to grow in Callie's chest. "Really?" she breathed, but knew it was so. She had seen for herself the growing respect of the locals and business owners. She had begun to make real friendships.

"And let me tell you something else, Callie," Louise said. "I made the biggest mistake of my life waiting all those years to say yes to Fred. I had some idea that I needed to remain loyal to the memory of your father, that it was all right to go out with Fred but to marry him would be like turning my back on your father and all we had shared. I had a hundred excuses every time Fred brought up the question of marriage. I'm just so lucky he didn't give up. I wasted so many happy years because I thought I needed to do 'the right thing.' I'm begging you not to make the same mistake. So what if one person or another thinks you married the man for his money or for what he could do for you? Somebody else might think he's marrying you for your beachfront property."

Callie laughed at that. Lu hooked arms with her and picked up the pace as they neared the old cottage. "The fact is, dear, will any of that matter in ten years or twenty years when you've shared laughter and tears and the birth of your children? Really, Callie, you aren't getting any younger, you know."

"I just hope I age as well as you, Mom," Callie said, noticing that the glow in Louise's eyes had little to do with the weather or the years. "You seem to get younger all the time."

"Married life can do that for you, Callie. Take my word for it, there's nothing that will age you faster than puttering around this old beach house alone day after day and night after night. Now what shall we fix for supper?"

10

WEDNESDAY MORNING Callie awoke to find surveyors pacing in front of her house. Her mother and Fred had left the night before to return to West Palm Beach. Callie needed to get into the office for at least a couple of hours before meeting Marlena for lunch. She was not expecting any surveyors.

"Good morning," she called to the team of men as she strode across the beach toward them. She had dressed as quickly as possible, all the while keeping one eye on their activities, and she wasn't at all happy with what she'd seen so far. "May I help you?"

One man tipped his cap and shook his head. "Thanks, no, we've got just about everything."

"Really. Do you mind telling me who you are and what you're doing surveying my land?" Callie's warm greeting had cooled at once.

The man seemed confused and looked at the others for help. "We're surveying this property," he repeated, and when Callie continued to stare at him added, "For the sale?"

"What sale?" Callie asked quietly.

"Well, the potential sale of this property to—" he consulted his clipboard, riffling through several pages

"—to . . . yeah, here it is, Mackin Properties. People hire us to analyze property for potential buyers and sellers. Then we give the clients our results and recommendations so they can decide whether or not to buy the property, or how much to sell for."

"Did Mr. Mackin hire you? Do you work for him?"

"Well, let's see." The man again consulted the clipboard. "According to my notes here, the report is to go directly to Mr. Mackin."

Callie had been so surprised when she heard the name Mackin that it took some time for her to digest what the man was telling her. When the light dawned, she looked back at him kindly. "I wonder if you could do me a favor. Could you send me a copy of your report?"

"Oh, that's automatic,' the man said, grinning. 'I mean, after all, there are two parties concerned here even though only one of you hired us. That would be Cal . . . lu . . ."

"Calusa," Callie supplied. "Barnes. Yes. Thanks."

The man smiled, tipped his hat again and rejoined his team. Callie was also smiling as she walked back to her house.

She spent the morning with Jerry going over the next several editions of the *Press*. In just six months Callie had brought it into competition with every small newspaper in Florida. In fact, more than one major state paper had courted Jerry and the other reporters in an effort to lure them away from the island.

She had to admit that she had come here to build a life
for herself—to find the individual so long buried in the
shadow of Sonny Martoni—and she had done it.

"Jerry, I'll be over at Island Pizza having lunch with
Marlena Davis if you need me," she called, and fairly
danced out the door, feeling very good about herself.

The pizza restaurant was small to begin with and
today it was teeming with customers. Callie saw
Marlena holding a small table near the window for
them and hurried to join her. "It seems this wasn't an
original idea," Marlena commented wryly, nodding
toward the lines at the bar and out on the porch. "I
ordered a medium cheese—hope that's okay."

Callie smiled and nodded. Just then she caught sight
of a familiar face across the room. Excusing herself,
she made her way around the tables to where Al
Mackin was sitting. She arrived just as he was down-
ing half a glass of beer, and he struggled to his feet to
meet her handshake when she spoke.

"Callie," he boomed, pumping her hand. "Have a
seat, little lady. I'll get you a beer." He was about to
call across the room to one of the harried waitresses
when Callie stopped him.

"I'm having lunch with Marlena Davis over there,"
she informed him, indicating the corner where Marlena waited, and Mackin waved a hand loaded with
a large slice of pizza in her direction. "Please don't in-
terrupt your lunch, Al." She paused long enough to

allow him to get the pizza into his mouth and take a huge bite before she said, "About the surveyors..."

Mackin choked and coughed loudly, reaching wildly for his beer. Callie pounded him none too gently on the back, asking sweetly if he was all right.

"Just went down the wrong pipe, little lady. Sorry."

"Well, now that I have your attention..."

Mackin had recovered enough to try to control the direction of the conversation. "Just a minute, Callie, I'm not sure what you're talking about here. Surveyors?"

"Let's don't play games, Al. We both know exactly what I'm talking about and for the record, my house is not for sale."

"Not even to Brookstone?" Mackin had a voice that carried in large halls. In the small restaurant it sounded as if he held a microphone, and Callie noticed several heads turning.

"Mr. Brookstone has not shown any interest in buying the house, but if he should I would tell him exactly what I'm telling you now," Callie said, maintaining her composure, her voice quiet and firm. "That house has been in my family for four generations and that's exactly where it's going to stay. Enjoy your lunch, Al."

When she got back to her table Marlena was grinning from ear to ear and silently applauding her with her eyes. "Callie, you were dynamite. People like that can take me apart in two seconds. I would have come slinking back here the minute he mentioned Mickey, but you were so—poised. No wonder Michael adores you so."

Callie wasn't sure how to answer that and was relieved when their pizza arrived at that moment. They ate in silence for a few minutes, but Marlena wasn't about to let go of her train of thought. "I know he's asked you to marry him. And you can tell me I'm out of line, but for the life of me, I can't figure out why you haven't said yes."

"Did Michael set this up?" Callie teased, and then became serious. "I love Michael, Marlena, and I know he loves me but I have to be sure that if we marry there will still be an individual me—a whole person rather than a part of him. Does that make any sense?"

"Are you concerned because of his family's position and wealth?"

"As a matter of fact, that is a part of it. Michael's responsibilities because of his family's position could get to be a big pain in the neck for us—others always after a piece of him, a piece of me because through me they think they'll get to him. I know that role too well, Marlena."

"But Mickey's crazy about you, Callie. You must know that. I mean before I met you, I was sure I was going to hate you—Mick made you seem so perfect. Do you know how many times a day that man talks about you? 'Callie says...' and 'Callie thinks...' It's pretty nauseating, you know." She grinned and Callie laughed.

"What about from my end? There you were Ms Perfectly Organized, Never-an-Eyelash-Out-of-Place while I slump around in sweatshirts and pigtails."

They entertained each other for several more minutes with stories of their mistaken first impressions of each other and then Marlena's face went serious. "You've got a lot of class, Callie. You've made such a place for yourself here on the island in such a short time. How could you possibly worry about ever being seen again as someone's shadow?"

Callie smiled but didn't answer. Instead she changed the subject. "How about stopping at Duncan's for cheesecake on the way back to work?"

"Why not?" Marlena agreed, letting the subject drop.

"OKAY, CALLIE BARNES, what spell have you cast over my assistant?" Michael's voice was teasingly gruff over the phone.

"What are you talking about?" It was after nine o'clock, and it was the first chance they'd had to talk all day.

"I mean Marlena comes back from lunch, tells me you leveled Al Mackin with a smile after he'd already fired his best shot and asks me when I'm going to marry Callie before someone else does."

"What did you say?"

"I told her she'd have to ask Callie that question, and you know what she said to that?"

"What?" Callie was smiling.

"She said she thought I should do the asking. And she said it with this lopsided grin that made me think she was onto something."

Callie laughed then and told him her version of what had happened with Mackin. She also related her talk with Marlena, her fears that a marriage to the Brookstone name would mean that she would once again cease to exist.

"It doesn't have to be that way, you know. You control whether or not you lose yourself, Callie," he whispered gently. "I think the reason it was so easy for you to disappear behind Sonny was because you didn't have much sense of who you were then. It was easier in a way to be Sonny's wife than someone you didn't even know yet."

"Perhaps," Callie agreed.

"And whether or not that's the truth, one fact remains. If you keep running from me or anyone else who loves you because you're afraid of what you will or won't be, then you've already lost yourself. As long as you have to hold me at arm's length, you're out of control. To be free you have to be able to make whatever decision you think will make you happy. What's the alternative—to keep up an affair for the next fifty years?" His laugh was warm and coaxing.

"There's a lot to work out," Callie said.

'There always is when two people plan to spend the rest of their lives together. I figure it'll take us just about that long to work it all out. So how about it?"

"How about what?"

"You want the full down-on-my-knees treatment?"

Callie smiled at the image. "Maybe."

"Okay, I'm on one knee—my bad knee—will you marry me?"

"I think I'd like that very much," Callie said softly.

Michael's whoop of joy raced down the telephone line. "I don't believe it," he yelled. "Callie? Get your calendar right this minute."

"Christmas?" she ventured.

"Too busy around here then. How about Thanksgiving?"

"You just don't want to wait until Christmas," she teased.

"Damned straight," he agreed. "How about tomorrow?"

"Gee, I have this meeting...."

"I'm coming over there right now. Don't move." And before she could reply the line went dead.

Callie hung up the phone and walked slowly around the office, shutting off all the lights except one small lamp on her desk. She curled into the corner of the ancient chintz couch that served as a waiting area for visitors to the paper. From there she could keep watch through the old blinds until she saw the lights of Michael's car. She saw him pull into the empty lot, then take the stairs two at a time before he threw open the door and strode into the office.

"Callie," he shouted, then seeing her waiting he repeated softly, "Callie." He locked the door and moments later they were in each other's arms, their hunger insatiable as their mouths locked in long moist kisses. The old couch groaned under their combined weight, but Callie was aware of nothing but the tantalizing roughness of his evening beard as it burned a trail from her lips to her neck.

"I love you, Callie," he murmured. His lips sought her breasts and his hands created exotic patterns on her thighs and hips.

Never had she wanted a man as she wanted Michael—all the time through all her waking and sleeping hours. Whenever he entered her she gladly would have spent the rest of her life holding him there inside herself. Yet, as much as she felt a part of him when they made love, she was sure of her separateness when they were apart, and that was good, too. He had allowed her the freedom to find herself. He had challenged and coaxed until she had blossomed into a confident, positive individual who knew herself and liked that person.

"Michael," she whispered against his ear, tasting the saltiness of him and the scent of the sea in his skin and hair, "I'm so scared."

He raised himself enough above her to look deeply into her eyes. "Of what?"

"It's so wonderful—us. What if something happens?" She knew she was being silly; there were no guarantees. One lived for the moment.

"Nothing will happen," he said with such a savageness that Callie looked again into the depths of his brown eyes and saw the reflection of the lamp like a flame, eternal and unwavering. "Nothing," he repeated, and buried his lips in her hair. When she held him in her arms it was easy to believe that.

"We're going to be just fine, Callie." Michael reached around and fished in the pocket of his jeans. "I've got something here."

Callie sat up, pushing her tousled hair away from her face, still feeling his lips on hers, still unable to keep her hands from caressing his muscled back and shoulders. "What?" she asked with only mild curiosity. She wanted only for him to come back and surround her once more.

"This," he said, and pressed into her hand a small blue satin box. "Open it." He watched her face as if wanting to memorize every nuance of her expression during the next minute.

"Michael," Callie said, breathing deeply. Nestled inside the box was the most incredible diamond ring she'd ever seen. The stones had been flawlessly set into the form of a fan shell raised above a gold setting that spread out into angel wings on either side. It was quite simply exquisite.

"Give me a date," Michael insisted, covering her hands with his own to prevent her from placing the ring on her finger.

"Thanksgiving?"

"You're sure?"

"I'm sure." She nodded, and he released her hand. He placed the delicate jewel on her finger himself.

"Just one request," he said, smiling, "if you're going to insist on being one of these modern women who keeps her own name, do you think you might permanently drop Martoni and just get back to Barnes?"

"I think I really like the sound of Callie Brookstone." It was the first time she'd dared to say it aloud, and she very much liked the sound of it.

Michael's smile faded as he caught her face between his hands and studied her in the dim golden light. "We are going to be so happy, Callie. I'll see to that."

"We'll see to it—together, Michael."

11

JERRY GOT UP and stretched. "Beautiful day," he commented, looking through the blinds at the cloudless sky. It was late September, but on the island the only hint of fall was the increased activity as everyone got ready for the season.

"Do you miss your New England autumns, Jerry?" Callie asked.

"Even after all these years, it's the one thing I do still miss. Don't miss the winters, mind you . . . but fall in Vermont . . ." He shook his head wistfully.

"Must be something," Callie said, remembering some Chicago falls that hadn't been so bad either. She hoped she and Michael would occasionally be able to get away to enjoy the changing of the seasons.

A voice interrupted the FM station's music and their own thoughts. ". . . tropical storm south of . . . could reach hurricane force...difficult to pinpoint whether storm will turn toward west coast...if it continues on its present track...Sanibel and Captiva directly in its path. . . ."

Jerry reached to turn up the volume, but the report was over after a warning to stay tuned for further developments. "A hurricane?" He turned to Callie as if to confirm his own hearing.

"It'll never hit here," she said. "Maybe Captiva, but this island wouldn't be lying in its path. Maybe we'll get a lot of wind and rain but not anything..." She was near to babbling as her thoughts raced with the possibilities of what a major tropical storm could mean to the island.

She and Jerry reassured each other and continued working while they told stories they had heard of the few storms that had touched the island in some major way. Callie remembered only one such storm. She was very small at the time and her memories were mostly of people scurrying around trying to get off the island before the storm hit. She could remember her parents were active in the evacuation efforts, and they were one of the last families to get away before the island was rocked by the full power of the thundering winds and rains. They had returned a day later to find their house had taken in a great deal of water and had some minor structural damage but was otherwise intact. Most important, there had been no injuries or loss of life on the island.

Jerry's memories were somewhat more vivid—the loss of communications, power and phone lines dangling, huge trees blown across the few roads that crisscrossed the island then. "There was very little development," he mused, obviously thinking of the enormous increase in population since those years.

"Well, if a storm should hit, at least this is a slow time. There aren't as many people to evacuate...." But Callie had already begun to consider the realities of moving tens of thousands of people off the two islands by means of a single two-lane road. "Jerry, we have to get something organized here. You call Ellie and Captain Jack. I'll get Michael and Chief Miller over here."

Within half an hour several island citizens were gathered in the paper's office. Captain Jack was explaining that regardless of the fact that the danger was not yet certain, evacuation should begin immediately. "The causeway could be covered by rising waters a full twelve hours before there's even a sign of rain or wind. We've got to allow for inexperience and panic. I say we start getting people out right now."

"But what if we're wrong? What if the storm turns in another direction?" asked a council member. "We're going to have a lot of angry people to deal with."

"Better a lot of angry people than a lot of dead bodies," Chief Miller muttered. "Jack is right. We need to start evacuation at once. I think we can reach the most people if we split up into teams. Callie, you and Jerry stay here and maintain phone contact with the mainland shelters." Within half an hour all the groups had left to carry out instructions. Chief Miller was going to station people at each end of the causeway and at every intersection along the evacuation route from the tip of Captiva to the causeway. He needed to recruit volunteers, and before leaving the office he had called each man and woman and given them their assignments.

By early afternoon Jerry and Callie could see a steady parade of vehicles moving down Periwinkle and off the island. It was still a sunny fall afternoon. Between calls they packed up files and equipment and loaded them into Jerry's old station wagon.

With difficulty, Callie persuaded Jerry to head for Fort Myers with the carload of materials. "I'll be fine, Jerry. As soon as the chief calls, I'm going to bike down to my place and put up the shutters. Then I'll meet Michael and we'll leave together."

"Don't try to be a hero, Callie," Jerry warned, studying her young face. "I mean it. Remember, the mainland may belong to man but the islands belong to the sea. Don't challenge her."

"I know." She looked out the window for a long moment. "It might not be the same two islands when we get back, will it, Jerry?" she said wistfully.

Jerry chuckled. "If this storm is what they're predicting, it could be twelve islands or none. One thing is certain." His face was very serious. "If even a piece of this one hits, there'll be a lot of rebuilding—a lot of starting over."

"Meet you here right after the all-clear?" Callie smiled at her friend.

"If there is a here, absolutely. Now get going. Call the chief. Call Michael. And get your buns off this place." He kissed her cheek and carried the last box out to his car. Callie stood on the porch and waved as he joined the parade of cars headed for higher ground and safety.

As she waited for the chief's call Callie checked the wall barometer. It was falling rapidly. The phone's ring was expected but it startled her nonetheless.

"Callie? Chief Miller. We're all clear here. Smooth sailing. Thanks to you and the others. Now get out of there."

"Have you heard from Michael?"

"Just had him on the CB. He's making one last cruise of the beaches in the Jeep just to be sure no one is left behind. Then he's headed for the office there to get you."

"Chief, can you get him back? Have him meet me at my cottage."

"All right, but don't stay there too long. Is your car there?"

"No. I'll bike there from here—it'll be faster."

"Okay. See you later."

Callie navigated her bike along the path becoming aware that tempers were beginning to fray. Horns beeped and several drivers shouted from their windows at other drivers or traffic controllers. She read the rising panic on the occupants' faces; they searched the sky as if the hurricane might appear any moment full-blown and sweep them out to sea.

She pulled her bike into the garage and raced up the stairs to the sun porch and into the house.

The memory of that one hurricane returned more vividly. She saw her mother and father racing through the house, securing hurricane shutters over every window until the inside of the house was dark as night. She tried to maintain her own calm while gathering emergency supplies—medical aids, jugs of drinking water, a large flashlight and a battery-operated radio. She searched the cabinets for simple foods that would require no cooking or refrigeration. She changed quickly into jeans, an old shirt and running shoes and stuffed her rain slicker into her duffel with the other supplies.

Outside she secured everything she could—the boat on the small canal, the lawn furniture, the grill, anything that could be moved or tied down. She loaded the water and other supplies into her car. Clouds raced across the gray sky and the wind whipped at her hair.

Satisfied that she had done all that she could, she ran back inside and called Michael's office. He should have been at the cottage by now, she thought. Maybe he had misunderstood and gone back to his office to wait for her.

Marlena answered the phone on the first ring. "He headed for the lighthouse over an hour ago, Callie. I thought he'd be at your place by now. Look, I have to get out of here myself."

"What about the lighthouse?" Callie asked.

"What about it?" Marlena sounded terrified.

"Are the shutters up on all the units?"

"How should I know?" The woman was practically hysterical. "Callie, I'm the only one left here. As far as I know every resident in any of our projects is safely off the island. It's eerie as all get-out here, and that's exactly what I intend to do—get out, right this minute. Good luck."

Callie raced down the stairs and headed for the lighthouse. Damn Michael. Time was getting short. It would be dark soon and the wind was rising. There was no way of knowing when the causeway would cease to be passable. She was certain that he was attempting to close up the lighthouse project without any help; he would never allow any of his men to stay behind when there was any danger—especially after Chicago.

Then she heard another radio bulletin, the announcer's voice fading intermittently. "...storm is now two hundred miles due...moving...the islands. Repeat. Get off the islands...causeway closing..."

Callie searched the now dark and somber sky as the first huge drops of rain spattered onto her windshield. It was becoming more and more difficult to hold her small car on course against the wind.

At the lighthouse she raced for the shopping complex calling Michael's name. His Jeep was parked near the old cypress but she saw no sign of him as she battled to stay upright in the gale. The surf pounding viciously against the shore drowned out her voice as she again called to Michael.

The shutters were mostly in place, and Callie realized he had started at the units closest to the road, working his way toward the beach. By the time she reached the last studio, the wind was pounding the building and water lashed at her. The waves were beginning to resemble a huge vanilla malt as they swirled higher and higher and closer to where she finally saw Michael wrestling with the last reluctant shutter. He could not budge it and was repeatedly being thrown against the building by the force of his own efforts and the wind. The rain was so thick in combination with the spray from the sea that momentarily Callie was disoriented, and within minutes she was completely soaked.

"Dammit, Michael," she muttered as she dropped to her hands and knees and crawled along the foundation. He continued to wage battle with the heavy shutter. Just as she reached his side he gave one mighty tug and the huge cover swung free. As he turned to lock it in place, though, the wind ripped it from its hinges. In what seemed like slow motion, Michael hurtled through the air, landing hard on the ground, the shutter crashing down on top of him. Callie looked on in stunned horror.

"Michael," Callie cried out, scrambling over to where he lay, completely still. She tore at the shutter and debris that covered him.

"Callie." His voice came out in a raspy whisper. He struggled weakly to help her move the board that pinned him, and at last they were able to budge it.

"Michael, what the devil...?" She was ranting and crying, frantically moving to free him completely. "Can you stand? Oh, Michael, if I have to carry you... Well, I will, that's all. I just will."

Groggily he lurched to his feet and leaned heavily against her. "Hi, darling, you look dreadful." He managed a smile.

"Shut up," she ordered tersely. "What the hell did you think you were doing...? Oh, my God...." He followed the direction of her wide-eyed stare.

Wedged through the windshield of her car was a large piece of roofing metal. Anyone in the front seat would have been killed instantly by the flying missile. "Let's get out of here, lady," Michael said, no longer seeing any humor in their situation. With her support he hopped as fast as he could to the Jeep. She got him settled and then raced to transfer supplies from her car to his. "Callie, leave that. Let's go," he yelled at her.

When she had maneuvered the four-wheel-drive vehicle onto the main road, she glanced over at him. "Just what the devil were you trying to prove?"

He started to explain, but she stopped him with a roar. "Don't talk. Thank God I caught Marlena. She told me you were here while she, being the smarter cookie, had the good sense to be scared out of her wits, wanting nothing more than to get out of here alive."

They sped past the road that led to the causeway, and Michael gripped her arm, his eyes wide with questions.

"Too dangerous," she shouted, sure the road would be partly submerged by now. "Not that staying here isn't," she muttered under her breath, navigating around a fallen tree. "Damned suicide being here now." Signs and garbage cans hurtled through the air in her path, and Callie felt like Rhett Butler trying to get Scarlett out of Atlanta while it burned.

When Michael's eyes closed, she shook him hard. "Don't go out on me. Just let me get you home. Does your leg hurt? There's some blood, but I don't think it's too bad." He saw that her hands shook whenever she loosened her iron grip on the wheel.

Callie could barely see a foot in front of her. She was driving as fast as possible, but their progress was slow. Then in the rain and gathering dark she thought she caught sight of a small beam of light. Before she realized it, she was almost on top of three teenage boys who were standing in the middle of the road desperately waving a weak flashlight at her.

"Get in," Callie screamed as she swerved to a stop beside them. Without a word the three piled into the back of the Jeep. They were soaked and dirty and terrified. "What are you doing still here?" Callie yelled above the storm.

One boy leaned across the back of the seat and spoke close to her ear. "We were camping, and when we heard the warnings we thought it would be neat to go down to the beach and see the waves and then we—"

"What! You thought you'd look at the waves? My Lord! Do you have any idea what a storm like this can do? No, I see you don't. Let's just say that it has the potential to level every condominium complex on the island if it hits in just the right spot."

Michael touched her arm, requesting a measure of restraint, but Callie was furious at the boys' stupidity and their total ignorance of what living on an island could mean.

"Then this is the real thing?" ventured another voice from the back. "A hurricane?"

"No, this is the warm-up. The hurricane should be here within the hour. You ain't seen nothin' yet."

"Callie." Michael's voice held a warning, and she knew she was scaring the already terrified youths even more.

"Are any of you hurt?" Callie asked, concern replacing the anger in her voice.

"No, ma'am," came three times from the back.

Callie smiled into the rearview mirror and continued in a brighter, more positive tone. "Good. When we get to the house, I'm going to need your help. If we do things right, we'll be able to ride out this storm and be here to brag about it."

She was searching for something positive for them to cling to through their fear. The truth was, they were a godsend; they could help her move Michael and get the house closed before the worst of the storm hit—if they were very calm and very lucky. With relief she saw their faces relax a bit as they fantasized about the stories they would have to tell.

"Mr. Brookstone is hurt, I'm not sure how badly. When we get to the house I want two of you to carry him inside and settle him on the floor nearest the inside wall in the dining room—away from any windows, okay? The other will come with me and the two will join us as soon as possible so we can batten down the hatches, so to speak. Understood?"

The chorus was instant and enthusiastic. "Understood."

The house trembled as Callie and the boys raced to secure it. Because it was on the bay side of the island, Callie thought it might be safe. In any case, it was their only chance. Using a flashlight to lead the way, Callie took the boys back into the dining room; the house was pitch black, without electricity. She knelt next to Michael and asked one of the boys to hold the light while she probed his injured leg.

At that moment the storm hit, all its fury seemingly directed at the five of them. They huddled together in the corner, the injured leg forgotten as torrential rains and wind howling like a banshee pummeled the house. Now and then they heard a crash and felt the structure shift on its foundation.

"Callie, are you scared?" Michael held her cradled against him and knew that the three boys were clinging tightly to each other, as well.

"Are you?" she challenged, and he felt the boys waiting for his answer.

"Damned straight," he breathed, and the five of them laughed softly, a bit nervously.

At times, the storm attacking the house sounded like twenty freight trains all headed at full speed for the dining room. But after what seemed a very long time, Callie decided to chance moving about to get some of the food, water and medical supplies. She had dropped everything in her rush to close the shutters in the living room.

"Stay put," she instructed, "I'll be right back." She began to crawl across the wide hall.

She thought the winds had died some but was aware that it might only be the eye of the storm. If that was the case, the winds would reverse and hit with equal force from the other side. The quiet after the raging noise was eerie, and Callie ran quickly toward the supplies, keenly attuned to every creak and moan of the house.

"Callie?" She heard Michael's concerned call from the other room.

"Coming," she called, grabbing the duffel bag and bending to collect the supplies, which were scattered on the floor. "Coming," she called again as she struggled to balance the awkward load and focus the flashlight. And then all hell broke loose.

With an ear-splitting shriek the wind tore through the stained-glass skylight, showering the living room with shards of colored glass. In seconds, everything from glass vases to lamps to tables had been set in a frenetic dance around the room. It looked like something Disney might have created except Callie knew this wasn't an illusion. Real objects—heavy objects—were flying around Michael's living room.

Her reaction time was a step slow; she paused for one split second too long to take in the strange sight before her. As she backed away into the hall a small end table sailed straight for her.

"Callie!" was the last thing she heard before she slumped unconscious at the foot of the winding staircase.

"No," Michael whispered, watching helplessly as she crumpled to the floor. He hobbled to where she lay and took her in his arms. "Callie?" He shook her gently. She was out cold. He checked her pulse and breathing. Both were steady. "Boys? Give me a hand here."

"Is Mrs. Brookstone going to be all right?" one of the teenagers asked as they carried her into the dining room.

"Mrs. Brookstone?" For just a moment Michael was confused. "Mrs. Brookstone will be fine. Help me get her settled, and one of you grab that food and water there." Yes, his Mrs. Brookstone was going to be just fine if he had anything at all to do with it.

They settled back into their corner of the dining room and waited for the winds to subside and the morning to dawn. Through the rest of the night Callie faded in and out of consciousness. Michael treated the large bump on her forehead as well as he could with the minimal supplies and lighting at hand.

Michael held her through the long hours and swore to himself that he would move heaven and earth to see that she was never in danger again if they could only get through this nightmare. Toward morning the storm finally started to wane and the three boys and Callie slept.

Her crusading spirit made sense to him now. What if there hadn't been people on the island who knew what a major storm could mean, who knew how to plan an evacuation, who knew what precautions to take? Callie had been right to come back and stir up everything and everyone on the island. He was beginning to be sorry he had wasted so much time fighting her before joining her wholeheartedly in her campaign.

"AT LEAST THE REST OF THE WEEK . . . nasty concussion . . . stitches out . . ."

Through her haze Callie heard an unfamiliar muffled voice. She strained to hear more and struggled to make her eyes open. They wouldn't, and she was trapped in the darkness. "Michael!" She screamed it, but knew it hadn't come out as more than the slightest movement of her lips.

She tried to put together the picture. She remembered being in Michael's house, the boys, the storm, then glass everywhere and tables and things flying through the air. Had someone found them now after the storm? Michael was hurt, or dead, and the boys . . .

Open! Silently she ordered her eyes and mouth to work. She licked her dry lips, and when at last she was able to open her eyes she found Michael standing in the doorway.

"Michael," she whispered, and tried to turn on her side. A wave of pain almost knocked her out again so she lay very still for several minutes and then tried again. This time she was able to sit up halfway.

"Hold it, Callie." Immediately Michael was beside her, easing her back onto the pillows. She was in his bedroom, which was filled with light—the light of a beautiful day. And Michael was seemingly whole, with the exception of a small white bandage over one eyebrow. She traced his features with her fingers and noted the toll the ordeal had taken on him. The lines around his eyes were deeper and he looked exhausted.

"Are you okay?" he asked anxiously.

"I'm fine," Callie answered with a smile, "but you look like hell."

He laughed at that, and she was relieved to see the softening effect it had on his features.

"What happened? I mean, after the skylight? How are the boys?"

"Safe and sound, back with their parents."

"How long have I been out?"

"Only two days."

"Two days!"

"Well, not quite. You were in and out. The storm finally blew itself out, and we brought you up here to the bedroom. One of the kids used the CB radio from the Jeep to radio for help."

"The cottage?" Suddenly Callie's eyes clouded, and she moved to get out of bed, but Michael caught her and pulled her into the circle of his arms.

"It didn't beat this storm, Callie. I'm sorry, babe." He held her for a long time and let her cry. When she had released her grief fully and lay against him with an occasional shuddering sigh, he told her the details of the storm. Twenty-foot water walls had battered the coastline, destroying several projects and homes and businesses. "A lot of people will be starting over, Callie. Places are just gone, piles of rubble where they originally stood. Kindling."

"And the lighthouse?" She steeled herself for his report.

"Thanks to some crazy lady who insisted on a steel substructure and then risked her life to help me get the shutters up, it survived. Oh, there's plenty of damage, but it's still standing. Callie, why did you come after me? If I had lost you... Dammit, Callie." He ducked his head against her shoulder but not before she had seen the tears well up in his soft brown eyes.

"I couldn't let you stay here and get killed for some stupid lighthouse. I knew it would tear you apart to lose that after all it had meant to us—after all you'd put into it...."

He shook her gently by the shoulders. "The only thing I'm afraid of losing is you. Do you understand that? And I'm not just talking about the storm. I'm also talking about this crazy idea you have that you're going to end up as my rib or something."

Callie laughed and stroked the lines from his worried face. "I think we've worked that out," she said.

"Speaking of which, you're quite a celebrity, you know. I'm not sure I can stand sharing you with your admiring public." He indicated the baskets of flowers that filled the bedroom.

"People are just being nice," she said. "Wait a minute. How did everybody know?"

"Ta da." With a flourish he presented her with a copy of the Fort Myers paper, then the Miami paper, then other papers from across the country. Her name and picture accompanied feature stories about her daring rescue of multimillionaire Michael Brookstone, and three island residents including—"'David Mackin, son of island developer, Al Mackin.' Michael? That was Al's son?"

"The same." He sat next to her again, presenting her with a single yellow rose from one of the arrangements. "That's not all. Mackin called. He's organizing some sort of banquet in your honor—wants to know when you'll be well enough to attend. Well, how does it feel?"

She tried to take it all in—the flowers, the publicity, the idea of a banquet. "I don't know," she murmured.

"I'll bet we won't be able to go into a restaurant or a shop without everybody coming over and wanting to talk with you and bask in your limelight. I'm just not sure I can handle that, Callie." His brow furrowed in a mock frown, but Callie saw the glint in his eye as his fingers played with the ribbons that would release the front of her gown.

"Stop that," she said, playfully slapping at his fingers. Callie hadn't thought about being a heroine. She had simply acted on instinct. But Michael was starting to explore her in very intimate ways, making further thought about the events of the past few days impossible.

"You know," he whispered as his tongue explored the curve of her ear, "we may just have to hire a social secretary to handle all of your obligations for the next year or so. You're going to be one busy lady."

"There's only one social event that I intend to concern myself with, Mr. Brookstone, and that's my wedding in November." She smiled and tugged him down next to her on the bed they would share for all their days.

A stranger's face.
A stranger's fate.
Or were they her own?

ANDREW NEIDERMAN

REFLECTION

They say everyone has a twin somewhere in time. Cynthia Warner finds hers in a photograph taken thirty years ago. Now she wonders if she will meet the same deadly fate as the woman in the picture...

ATTRACTIVE, SPACE SAVING BOOK RACK

Display your most prized novels on this handsome and sturdy book rack. The hand-rubbed walnut finish will blend into your library decor with quiet elegance, providing a practical organizer for your favorite hard-or soft-covered books.

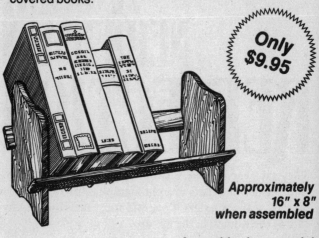

Only $9.95

Approximately 16" x 8" when assembled

Assembles in seconds!

To order, rush your name, address and zip code, along with a check or money order for $10.70 ($9.95 plus 75¢ postage and handling) (New York residents add appropriate sales tax), payable to *Silhouette Reader Service* to:

In the U.S.

Silhouette Reader Service
Book Rack Offer
901 Fuhrmann Blvd.
P.O. Box 1325
Buffalo, NY 14269-1325

Offer not available in Canada.

BKR-2